FRIENDS WITH BENEFITS

BRITS IN MANHATTAN BOOK THREE

LAURA CARTER

Boldwood

First published in 2018. This edition first published in Great Britain in 2023 by Boldwood Books Ltd.

Cover Design by Rachel Lawston

Cover Illustration by Rachel Lawston

This book is a work of fiction and, except in the case of historical fact, any resemblance to actual persons, living or dead, is purely coincidental.

Every effort has been made to obtain the necessary permissions with reference to copyright material, both illustrative and quoted. We apologise for any omissions in this respect and will be pleased to make the appropriate acknowledgements in any future edition.

A CIP catalogue record for this book is available from the British Library.

Paperback ISBN 978-1-78513-550-7

Large Print ISBN 978-1-78513-549-1

Hardback ISBN 978-1-78513-548-4

Ebook ISBN 978-1-78513-551-4

Kindle ISBN 978-1-78513-552-1

Audio CD ISBN 978-1-78513-543-9

MP3 CD ISBN 978-1-78513-544-6

Digital audio download ISBN 978-1-78513-546-0

Boldwood Books Ltd
23 Bowerdean Street
London SW6 3TN
www.boldwoodbooks.com

1

JAKE

16 Years Ago

School is out but, like every day, I'm standing in the yard, kicking up dirt with my scuffed shoes, waiting for Emily. She always takes ages. I don't know what she does after the bell rings but she's never out on time. Me, I get out of there as soon as I can, especially on a Friday. It's like she actually enjoys being at school.

'Ah, look, Jake's waiting for his girlfriend again.'

That's Tommy 'no-good-for-nothing' Arnold. The biggest jackass in school. He was a nobody before the growth spurt last year that made him three inches taller than everyone else. He was already ten inches wider. Fat ass!

'Get stuffed, Tommy,' I say, letting him hear the boredom in my voice. It's the same-old-same-old every night, except for Wednesdays, when Emily has gymnastics class and her mom picks her up.

Tommy has his group of followers around him. Some of them are decent guys. I play football with most of them. He's too out of shape to play himself so he pretends he's too cool for it. He's not.

'Yeah, what you gonna do, Jake? Cry about it with your girlfriend?'

I take a deep breath through my nose and shake my head. He's not worth it.

Bored of not getting a rise out of me, he heads off in the direction of home, punching one of the guys in the arm and no doubt trying to get a reaction out of him. It's like Mom says: one of these days, Tommy will be fat, bald and stupid, so the joke's on him.

'Finally!' I call when I see Emily making her way out of the school doors with two friends. They all have blonde hair and the same two pigtails braided down either shoulder. They all have on similar pink dresses and those bright princess backpacks they wear.

She beams when she sees me, like she always does, as if she isn't expecting me to be waiting for her. In return, I give her a smile that lifts only one side of my mouth. I learned it from my brother, Drew. He's almost ten years older than me and he's pretty cool, not that I ever tell him as much. Apparently, it's a hit with the ladies, his lazy smile. I'm not sure why I do it around Emily. I guess I'm practicing on her for when I meet real chicks.

'Bye, girls!' Emily calls, waving off her friends while running to me. 'Hey, Jakey.'

I want to be mad at her for being late, again, but I can't. She's just a kid. She's two years younger than me, only eight. And she's short, you know. I'm a protector of sorts. That's what Mom says, anyway. That's why I have to walk her home every day. That, and the fact we live on the same street, so it makes sense.

We walk back along the sidewalk, which is speckled with sand from the gusts we've had on the island the last few days, blowing up from South Shore Beach. It's one of the things I love about Staten Island: always being close to the beach.

'What did you do at school today?' I ask her.

'Mm...' She looks to the sky as she thinks.

'Emily, your lace is untied.'

She shrugs and keeps walking. I come to a halt on the sidewalk.

'Stop and tie your lace or you'll hurt yourself.'

She breathes out huffily but bends to fasten her lace. 'You're so bossy,' she grunts at me.

'Yeah, well, you'd be calling me worse names if I let you fall and break your arm.'

'That wouldn't happen. You have to fall off a cliff or something to break your arm.'

'Oh, really? How would you know?'

She shrugs again but stares at her toes when she stands. I hate when she does this. It makes me feel like a douche. 'Look, how about I race you home?'

Although she doesn't lift her head, I can see from the way the sides of her face lift that she's smiling. I know any second now, she'll turn and run. And she does.

'You cheat every time!' I shout.

I catch up to her, but not before she runs smack into Tommy Arnold, who's deliberately stepped in her way.

It happens in a heartbeat. She looks up. Tommy pushes her back and she stumbles to the ground. As she does, his eyes are on me. Tommy doesn't care about Emily. He wants to pick a fight with me because I'm the popular kid and the only person Tommy needs to take out to be king of the jungle.

'What do you think you're doing?' I snap at him as I help Emily to her feet.

'I'm okay.' She sniffs.

I lift her chin and see her tears. I don't know why but they throw me into some kind of rage. I can't see straight, or think straight. I can only imagine putting my knuckles in Tommy Arnold's face.

When I turn to him, he's already taking a swing at me. But he's slow and clumsy. I block his arm and put all my strength into my fist as I drive a punch into his nose. He rocks back but doesn't fall. The rest of his group backs away, clearly wanting to see how this pans out before picking a side.

'Go home,' I tell Emily. I can see our street from here. She'll be fine.

'No. I won't leave you, Jakey.'

Tommy laughs, hard and nasty. 'Jakey. Jakey. Should we pick flowers together, Jakey?'

'Go, Emily. I've told you.'

She starts to move but Tommy blocks her, putting his forearm against her neck.

Now he's really overstepped.

I drive my whole body into him, taking us both to the ground.

'Go, Emily!' I shout one last time.

As I watch her leave, Tommy gets an elbow into my nose. I shake my head, shaking off the blow. Then I find some superhuman strength and hold his neck, pinning him down as I smash my fist into his cheek.

'Don't ever call me Jakey. And don't dare touch her again. You got that?'

His head lolls to the side and blood starts to come out of his nose but he nods.

I get off him because I've made my point. I hate him. I hate that he dared to go near Emily and that I let him, when I'm supposed to be looking after her. But I know he won't be bothering either of us again.

As I walk away, some of the other kids call to me.

'That was awesome, Jake!'

'We knew you'd smash him, Jake.'

I hear a few bad names being hurled at Tommy and I couldn't care. He deserves it. Maybe next year, he won't start off being a jackass.

When I get home, Mom is in the front yard with my brother and his best buddy, Brooks. Emily is clinging to Mom's legs.

'See, he's just fine. You run along home now, Emily.'

Emily leaves my mom's side and rushes toward me on the driveway. 'Your nose is bleeding.'

She reaches up to touch my face but I clock the looks my brother and Brooks are wearing and pull back from her. 'Go home, Em.'

'I'm sorry, Jake. This is my fault.' She starts to sob.

I look from my mom to Drew, then to Brooks. 'It's not your fault, Em. Tommy wanted to pick a fight with me. Go home.'

'No. I can't leave when—'

'Go home!' I shout.

She cries harder but heads down the street toward her house.

I close my eyes, bracing myself for the tongue lashing from my mom, and when I open them, she is standing right in front of me.

'Look at this,' she says, raising her hand to my cheek and rubbing her thumb under my nose. 'Are you going to tell me what happened?'

I pull her hand away from my face, conscious my brother is watching us. 'Yeah, Tommy Arnold got what was coming to him. Can I go inside?'

Surprisingly, she takes a step back. I raise my chin to Drew and Brooks as I pass by.

'Proud of you, man,' Drew says, making my stride falter.

Brooks' hand comes down on my shoulder. 'Getting in a fight over a chick is like a rite of passage, man. Don't feel bad.'

My mom walks beside me, insisting I come inside to get cleaned up. I follow her into the house.

'Hey, Jake!' Brooks calls before I close the door. I turn to face him. 'You should come to the gym with us sometime. We can teach you a few extra moves.'

I try to stay cool but I know I end up grinning. 'Yeah, maybe.'

2

JAKE

Now

I'm standing in a bar in Covent Garden, drinking a pint of English ale. A new ale to me. Apparently, it was brewed in Cornwall, which I'm told is on the south coast somewhere. It's smooth. Creamy. Maybe a new favorite. The Brits love their ale, I should tell you that.

I've been living in London for two years now, since I took a job at a hedge fund over here, right out of college at NYU. Why am I here in London? That's a long story and one I don't feel like getting into right now because it's Saturday night and I'm enjoying beers with the guys. Well, guys *and* girls who keep coming over to talk to us, same difference.

'That one there is absolutely gagging for it.' The source of those words, leaning into my ear, is one of my roommates, Alex. He's a pompous twat, as the Brits say. Speaks like the royals but give him one beer and he has none of their grace. His full name is Alexander Frederick Embersome-Evrington the Third. But God love him. He's a giant goof ball too. If he likes you, truly likes you, he'll move heaven and earth for you. Or pay someone to do just that.

Now, he's pointing to a leggy blonde. No meat on her bones. Not much shorter than me at six two. She's sporting a face full of makeup and a sequin dress as short as the type Taylor Swift wears. It's out of place in the old English pub but I'm guessing she's headed from here to a club in Soho.

'I'm bagging this one,' Alex tells me, totally self-assured, and is probably right to be.

'Go get your Saturday night,' I tell him.

Leaning back against the bar, I watch him make a move, working his magic.

My buddy, Sean, turns from the bar and hands me another beer, so I'm double parked. I drain my first as I accept the second.

'How does he do it?' he asks, as the blonde giggles and falls happily under Alex's arm.

Charlie, a guy I work with, extricates himself from blondie's friends and joins our conversation. 'Alex is unbelievably obnoxious, yet he pulls the hottest women every time. Maybe I'll start acting like a knob head twenty-four-seven.'

I laugh because it's both true and well-meant. 'It's that baby-blond, preppy-boy look,' I tell them.

'If I ever have a son, I'm sending him to boarding school to give him a start in life. The ladies love it.'

We all banter with each other a lot but we all have each other's backs: Alex, Charlie, Sean and me. We make up four of our usual Saturday night six-some. Charlie and Sean were the first guys I met when I moved across the pond. Charlie was working all kinds of jobs – mostly bar work – to supplement his income whilst he gains traction as a stand-up comedian in London's comedy clubs.

Sean is a snooker player. A pro snooker player. He and Alex are childhood buddies and tried to hustle me one night. Charlie knows Sean from all the bar work and Charlie is possibly the worst snooker player the world has ever seen.

The other two of our six-some are Jess and Abby. I live with Jess. She's awesome. I mean, certifiably nuts, but such a laugh. And Abby is Sean's much finer other half. She's hot as hell and always looks stunning, even if you catch her on an errands day. I guess she feels like she has to make an effort all the time since she's had years of being pictured in magazines with Sean. Generally, though, they do all right when they're out. By that, I mean they don't usually get recognized unless some guy knows his snooker well.

The girls will be here shortly. Jess is taking part in a fashion show tonight in which Abby is modeling. Jess designs clothes and accessories, which she sells in boutiques around the city. Her brand name is slowly getting out there, helped by her regular fashion column in a free magazine they give out on the city's underground system. Tonight, it's only her accessories being used by other clothes designers but it's still great publicity.

'Hey Jake, did you go check out some bikes today?' Sean asks.

I swallow the ale in my mouth. 'I did. I saw a sweet Harley. I'm torn between that and the Yamaha I saw last week.'

'I'll never understand motorbikes,' Charlie says. 'It's suicide. Especially in the city. Driving a car in the city is bad enough. In any case, you can't really get your speed up. Where's the fun?'

'It beats the traffic. Plus, I can take her out on a weekend and tear up some dirt,' I tell him.

'You're crazy, do you know that?'

I chuckle. 'Yeah, you tell me nearly every day.'

'You should think about it, Charlie,' Sean says. 'Might help you and that ginger mullet pick up a woman.'

'First, it's strawberry blond. Secondly, you don't know what you're talking about. Ginger is in,' Charlie counters.

'He's right, Sean. Ed Sheeran and Prince Harry have made red cool.' Sean looks from me to Charlie, seeming to contemplate the not-at-all-serious discussion seriously. Then he says, 'Nah, I don't buy it. You'll always be a ginger loser to me.'

We're all laughing when a slender hip bumps into me accidentally on purpose as its owner flutters her eyelids, moving away from the bar with a glass of rosé in her hand. 'I'm sorry about that,' she says.

I subtly give her a once-over: her tight, white jeans, her black, fitted vest that fastens by one button at her navel, and under which she's sporting nothing but a push-up bra. Too obvious. But she did make the effort so I'll kill ten minutes on her.

'You always this clumsy?' I ask, twisting to face her.

She giggles like an airhead: high-pitched and way too overzealously. 'Not always. Only when I'm in a fluster. Hey, is that an American accent?'

After giving up on trying to hear her name above the music and spending ten minutes listening to her tell me how much she'd love to visit Manhattan one day, I'm checking my watch. Sean and Charlie have found a couple of guys we know, Cash and Will, and have no intention of rescuing me. Alex seems to have disappeared with the blonde. Most likely to her place or the bathrooms; he's a swift mover.

Come on, Jess, I think.

As if in answer to my call for help, I see Jess making her way up the stairs and into the bar with Abby.

I motion to the bartender and when I have his attention, I order a glass of pinot noir for Jess and a sem-sauv for Abby.

'Sorry, babe, it's been good talking to you but I've got to go. Make sure you see Manhattan one day,' I tell the irritating girl as I move away from the bar.

Sean gets to Abby and Jess at the same time I do. After I give the girls their drinks, Sean steals Abby away.

When I'm left with Jess, I look her up and down, not subtly at all. She's wearing skinny jeans with turn-ups. She has on bright-red heels – killer heels that make her already fine legs more than three inches longer – which have a small red and white check bow on the side, secured with a black button. I recognize the design as one of hers. I trail my eyes up to her blouse. In true Jess style, it's quirky, maybe even a little outrageous, but not as much as some of her stuff. This is a chiffon blouse, layers of red, black and white fabric. For all the layers, the cut of the top brings it in at the waist and it sits neatly over her perfectly formed breasts, dipping just enough to give a teasing glimpse of her cleavage.

Her long, brown hair has been pinned loosely and a few rogue strands hang down. I consider her face. She pouts for me, displaying her bright-red lipstick. Her eyes are natural-looking but darkened with liner.

Her cheeks have been bronzed but not overly so. In one ear, she has a gold stud. In the other, one dangling leaf.

'So?' she asks, sipping her pinot.

I rock my head from side to side, as if deliberating. 'Show me your bag.' She holds up a black clutch; I know the style because she's told me before. The top of the purse is folded like an envelope, the triangle red, with a button to match her shoes. 'I'd say you're like a seven.'

'Seven? I'll take it!'

I try not to let my smile show. My night just improved ten-fold. Jess is my favorite person in England. My reason for being here these days, I guess you could say.

'How was the show?'

'Not bad. I think I have an order from one of the designers.'

'That's awesome.' I hold up my ale. 'To you.'

'Cheers.' I love how she says that. It's so British. So Jess. 'Are you going to give me the lowdown? I saw the woman with the big boobs you were talking to when I arrived.'

I shake my head as I take a drink. Then I say, 'Airhead.'

'That's never stopped you.'

'You think very little of me.'

'Babe, don't be offended. That's just because I know you.'

Laughing, I tuck her under my arm and we make our way over to Sean, Abby and Charlie.

'We've already lost Alex to a too-skinny blonde with legs the length of Niagara,' I tell her.

'The length of Viagra?'

I look down to her, taller even with her in her heels, and roll my eyes. 'You can do better than that.'

'That's fair. I'll try harder.'

Harder. Ha.

'Is there another bad joke coming?' I ask.

She smirks and I know she's focused on the word *coming*. I know because I am too. *Viagra. Harder. Coming.* I almost groan.

An hour later, we find Alex on the dancefloor in a Soho club. He's holding on to the woman's hips as she grinds her ass into his crotch.

Jess clinks her gin and tonic against mine. It's that time of night; we've switched from wine to clear spirits. 'All right, Jakey, let's play.'

'What's the bet?'

She turns on the spot. I know she's considering the women in the club. 'Her. There. Pretty black dress. Pink lips. Wavy, dark hair.'

'She's hot.'

'She is. I bet you can't get her number in the next five minutes.'

I drain the gin in my glass. 'Five minutes?'

I assess the girl. She looks confident. She's very attractive. You might think that would give me less of a chance. But the thing is, I know women. I know that the most attractive women don't get chatted up like their more average-looking friends. Good looks intimidate men, make them think, 'Why would I put myself out there in a club for what is probably no more than a one-night stand, and risk being turned down in front of my friends?' And they ultimately decide there's no reason to try. They're safer betting on plainer women. But that's why, when you do talk to the pretty girl, she's flattered. That's why I'll win this bet.

'Deal,' I say, turning back to Jess. 'Best get yourself a tequila shot ready.'

I move off, feeling Jess's eyes burning into me. The girl in the little black dress is laughing with a group of friends. She's more attractive up close. I only have five minutes, so after checking that the fourth finger of her left hand is jewelry free, I go right in for the kill. I slide my hand along the small of the girl's back but I don't speak to her first, I speak to her friends. That's the in. Let the friends do some of the hard work for you. Let them smile approvingly. Get their attention. Then let the target know that, despite all her friends, who usually get chatted up, you want her.

'Evening, ladies.' Cue the smile. 'It's quite clear to me you're having a sophisticated girls' night.' The compliment. 'But I couldn't help noticing your friend here from across the bar.' Now I look at the target and turn my big smile to a half, sexier smile. 'Hi, I'm Jake.'

Her eyes widen a little. I've nailed her right on. She's surprised by my approach. 'Aria,' she says, holding out her hand. I take it but kiss her cheek.

'That's a beautiful name. Is it British?'

'Actually, my parents are Irish and Italian.'

'Ah, I thought there was something a little exotic about you.' I turn back to her friends. 'I don't want to interrupt your night. And I'm not the kind of guy who thinks you find anything lasting in a club.' I see the swooning look about her friends' faces. 'But, if it's okay with you, Aria, I'd like to take your number. Maybe I could take you out sometime?'

Her cheeks seem to flush. I've gotten to her. Which means I'll also be walking away with her number.

When I get back to Jess, she's already holding her shot of tequila in one hand and a lime in the other. 'You're too smooth-talking for your own good, Jake.'

I flash her a wink and tell the bartender to set down another shot. I can't let her drink alone.

We each lick salt from our hands then Jess counts us down. 'Three, two, one.'

Tequila. The burn. Lime.

'Ah, that stuff never gets better,' I say, laughing at Jess's screwed-up face and the way she bangs a foot on the floor.

'Time to dance?' she asks, once I'm convinced her shot is staying down.

We move into the crowd of sweating people drunk dancing. I take Jess's hand, making sure she's with me as we find the others. Abby immediately accosts her so I start dancing around like a fool. A fool who is high on life.

I do the running man. The dancing bear.

I watch Jess move, her head dropped back, her arms above her head. She looks happy. Carefree. And – I can say this because we're friends – damn hot.

Some guy obviously agrees because he worms up to her, his hands around her waist. His crotch against her ass. She smiles but lifts his hands from her hips. He doesn't take the hint, reaffirming his grip. She tries to wiggle free. When it doesn't work, her eyes meet mine.

I step toward her and take her hands, tugging her to me. Glaring at the jerk behind her, I tell him, 'Take your fucking hands off my girlfriend.'

The guy quickly shifts his attention from Jess to me, looks me up and down, I suspect realizing I'm six two and seeing that I'm ripped beneath my black shirt, since it's fitted and tucked into my gray slacks. He holds up his hands and backs off.

I pull Jess tighter and she slots her legs either side of mine, fitting me like a glove. It's not like we're not up for dirty dancing; we just don't want to dirty dance with sweaty, pissed-up strangers. It's kind of an agreement we have. If one of us is stuck with someone in a bar or a club, we pull out the boyfriend or girlfriend card. Most often, it's me telling men to keep their paws off her but sometimes it cuts the other way.

The track changes to one of Bieber's latest tunes and I know Jess will ramp up the moves. She loves Bieber, no matter how much I tell her that at thirty, she's too old for him. I will admit that his latest stuff isn't awful. But I'd never say that to her.

I hold her waist as she leans back, her arms waving, her hips grinding into me. We dance together until she calls time for another shot.

The bartender sets alight to two shots of Sambuca on the bar. I count us in this time and we shoot. The fire heats my throat and tips me over the edge from friendly drunk to horny. I watch Jess's neck as she swallows, knowing how good her skin tastes. Knowing that when she's had Sambuca, our nights together are sensational.

She brings her head forward and opens her eyes to mine. As if we're completely in sync, which we usually are, I can sense that her lids are heavy. Her pupils dilate. 'Is it home time?' she asks.

I take her shot glass and step to her as I place it on the bar. I drag my hands down her back and roughly pull her hips into me. 'It's home time.'

She laughs, the sound reverberating against my lips. 'So serious.'

'Making sure you get home to bed is no laughing matter.'

On the street, we try to flag a cab but none of them have their lights on. We head down to Embankment and start walking by the Thames in the direction of home, our conversation interspersed with the kind of kisses that make me want to speed up the journey.

By the time we make it to our building, I'm so desperate for her, my fly might pop. She unlocks the apartment door. The lights are out and there's no noise. Alex is still out, or maybe not coming home.

I pick her up, wrapping her legs around my waist, and hastily press her back against the door, devouring her mouth as she frantically unbuttons my shirt. She wants this as much as I do. It's hardly a surprise. Our sex is out of this world.

The best part of sleeping with your best friend is that you can tell each other exactly what you want.

* * *

I wake under the heat of London's sun, even though my blind is drawn. That's the first clue that it's late morning. Starfish on my bed, on top of the sheets, I shake my head quickly from side to side, assessing the extent of my hangover. I'm groggy but I've had worse.

The next thing to hit me is the sound of... what is that? Waves? Crashing waves?

In case I need to state the obvious, there should not be crashing waves in the center of London city. I grumble to myself as I drag myself up to sit. After taking ten seconds to come around, I push myself to my feet and find a pair of sweatpants to pull on.

As I walk the corridor, the sound changes to something like animals in a jungle. I notice Alex's bedroom door is open and his bed made. I assume he stayed out last night.

As I near the living room, I'm struck by the smell of burning bacon.

When I open the door, the light from the floor-to-ceiling windows makes me squint. Jess is sitting in the middle of the living room, on the rug. She's wearing yoga pants and a T-shirt. Her legs are crossed beneath her and her hands resting on her knees. Her eyes are closed and I notice her iPhone in the docking speakers, which I can only guess is where the sound of a howler monkey is coming from.

'What are you doing?' I ask.

'Shh, I'm trying to get back into meditation.'

'Christ. Another fad. Why do I smell burning bacon?'

'Oh, fuck.' She springs up from the rug and runs to our small kitchen. I follow her in as she takes a grill tray from the oven. The fat of the English bacon – not streaky like in the US – is crispy but not altogether destroyed. 'Help yourself,' she says. 'I'm having a meat day today because I'm trying out vegan for a week starting tomorrow.'

I move behind her, threading my arms through hers to grab a piece of crispy pig. 'Why in God's name are you trying vegan and meditating?'

She turns in my arms, her back pressed to the kitchen counter. 'I'm finding myself,' she says, laughing as she bites the end of a piece of bacon.

'Seemed like I was finding you last night.'

She pushes my chest and sets about making us bacon 'butties' in her words. A buttie is just a bread roll. I don't get why she calls it that. It's a Jess-ism, I guess. 'You don't need to find me. You know me.'

'Very true.'

'I'm going to a tai chi class later. You want to come?'

'Absolutely not. Thanks, though.' I take a buttie from the plate in front of her and head into the living room. 'Can I turn off the monkeys?'

'Yeah, I'm sufficiently cleansed for the day, I think.'

She comes into the room and nestles into one corner of the sofa, opposite me. 'Formula One okay?' I ask, fishing the TV remote from behind the sofa cushion.

'Mm.' She nods, chomping down on her food. 'For sure.'

I flick on the flat-screen and we spend the next hour watching Hamilton thrash everyone else on the course.

The other great thing about our arrangement is that there's no awkward next day. There's never a question of whether one of us wants more. She's emotionally scarred and I'm too sensible to be burned by a woman again. End of.

3

JAKE

Ah, Mondays. The reason God made Friday night, Saturday and Sunday; he felt so bad about creating Monday.

I set my takeout coffee cup down on my desk and boot up the inevitable: a full inbox. Don't get me wrong, I don't hate my job. In fact, I love working for one of the world's largest hedge funds. It just takes me a while to get going on a Monday morning, that's all.

Before taking a seat, I hang my suit jacket on the hook in my office, dump my gym stuff in a drawer, and look out over St James's Park. Have I mentioned that my office has a killer view? Well, I do. And because I am in the office before the London stock markets open for trading, I get to watch people waking themselves up with a morning run, a dog walk, a coffee and stroll.

It may have been a last-minute choice to change from the New York office of Gold Rock Investments to London, but I am glad I made the decision. London is like New York in so many ways. Tall buildings, busy lives. But it seems brighter somehow. Less claustrophobic. And I think it's funny watching the kind of Brits you find in the Chelsea and Kensington Borough... the kind I work for... walking with a pole so far up their 'arse', they look like toy soldiers.

The best thing about London, though, is that I haven't been betrayed here. Sure, I miss my folks out on Staten Island. I miss my brother and friends. But here, I'm not reminded every day of the girl I loved and lost.

'Here he is: my best trader.' Marcus Benedetti, also known as my boss, comes into my office. 'For you.' He sets a white envelope on my desk. 'Great month, last month.'

As he heads back out of my office, he asks me if I had a good weekend, his words coming from along our eighth-floor corridor. I don't bother answering.

Instead, I sit at my desk, pulling up the NASDAQ exchange on one of my three screens, the FTSE on another, and my inbox on the third. I see the headline of an email that names me as the highest earner for the fund last month. Some months you win, some months you lose. I've been lucky that my bets on commodities and other alternative investments have been paying off lately.

Kind of pleased with myself, I pick up the envelope Marcus left and lean back in my chair. I have five minutes until the FTSE opens. I slide out the letter and open it. My eyes immediately bulge as I gawp at the number of zeros printed on the check. I've had bonuses before but this... this is N.I.C.E.

Dragging a hand back through my dark hair, I exhale. Who'd have thought I'd be making this kind of money three years into my career? Little more than three years ago, I was tending a college bar. Now, this...

At seven fifty-nine, I interlace my fingers and stretch my arms out in front of me as I prepare for the exchange to open.

By lunchtime, I have tracked my highest risk investments, put client money into energy markets I expect will prove highly lucrative, and I'm ready for a break.

There's a sushi bar on the ground floor of the building and there's a large sashimi salad with extra wasabi that has my name all over it. I pull on my suit jacket – black because Jess tells me my tanned skin and dark hair mean I can pull it off – and adjust my shirt collar. We don't wear ties in the office. We aren't as pompous as lawyers and accountants.

Given it's close to 2 p.m., there isn't a huge line. That's why I've trained my body to crave food at this time. I pay for my salad – does it count as a salad if it's full of fish and rice? – and make for the self-serve counter to pick up chopsticks and a napkin. Except I can't pick up chopsticks and a napkin because Natasha is standing between me and my cutlery, leaning back against the counter, the glint of 'let's go to bed' in her eyes.

I can confirm that Natasha looks good in, and out, of clothes. But she's as loose as a slipknot. I only ever broke my rule and went back for seconds because she's very good at yoga, and all that implies.

And yes, I do go for seconds with Jess too. But let me get one thing straight. Don't think I make an exception to my rule for Jess because she's the one or something. Jess and I have an arrangement. We've had an arrangement since a drunken night on the sofa two months ago, when we were both feeling horny but wanted to have sex with no strings, and with someone who could understand what we each want.

Back to Natasha, and the fact she has put the tip of her index finger into her mouth as she wraps her hand around her lower waist, drawing my attention to her hips beneath her skintight pencil skirt. 'I haven't seen you down here for a while, Jake.'

I signal for her to move aside so I can get my chopsticks. 'Then you mustn't have been around because I'm down here almost every day at the same time.'

She giggles, despite the fact I wasn't joking. 'Right. Listen, I'm having a girls' night with a few friends this Saturday. We're going out on King's Road. You'd be welcome to come say hi.'

I pull off the white paper packet from my chopsticks, bending around her to use the trash can. 'Wouldn't that defeat the point of having a girls' night?'

She giggles again. There's not much between the ears with this one. 'Right. Well, maybe you could bring some friends. We could make it a mixed group.'

'Sounds great but I'm in New York this weekend.' I start to walk away.

'New York? New York with who? I love New York.'

I lose the sound of her voice as I step onto the marble floor of the lobby and out through the revolving door to Pall Mall. The sun is out, lighting up the beige stone buildings. Pall Mall is my favorite street in

London. You would think I'd dislike it maybe, because I work here, but it reminds me of Wall Street, Lower Manhattan. Home.

Maneuvering through suits running to meetings and talking into cell phones, then navigating the traffic, I head down Marlborough Street and cross the road to wander into St James's Park. I find a free bench and take a pew, leaning forward across my knees to finally dive into my bowl of protein. This is a lunch that would win the approval of Brooks, who is a fitness trainer and nutritionist to the rich and famous in NYC.

As I have that thought, I remind myself to transfer the bonus I got this morning to my mom's bank account.

My parents think I don't know that my brother paid for my college tuition.

I'm not saying I'm unloved. I was definitely loved. But it's no secret I was also a mistake. I'm the youngest of three. Drew is almost ten years older than me. My sister, Millie, is eight years older.

Anyway, they had me and they gave me everything I needed, but definitely not everything I wanted. I was far from spoiled. But they gave me all they could. When it came to college, though, it would have cost them their retirement fund to send me. So, I know Drew paid for my tuition and that they have some kind of pact to keep it secret. I think it's a pride thing.

I'll thank Drew one day. For now, I transfer money to Mom's account to 'pay my parents back.' Knowing them, they'll pass the money right on to Drew. Drew won't want it. They'll argue. Eventually, my mom will win because she always wins. She's Mom. Heart of gold, determination of a gladiator.

'Excuse me, do you mind if I sit?'

I take my eyes from the salmon nipped between my chopsticks and follow the bare legs of what I can only describe as a MILF.

I do a quick assessment. No ring on the fourth finger of her left hand but a beast of a rock on the fourth finger of her right hand. I'd stake money on her being a divorcee. And since I gamble for a living...

'Please, take a seat. I'd enjoy the company.'

She nods, shyly, but flashes me a small smirk. Cheeky. Foxy.

'American?' she asks, as she sits, crossing one of those fine legs over the other beneath her tailored dress.

'New York. You don't sound like a Londoner.'

'Ah, no. I'm from Manchester originally.' She tucks a loose tendril that's fallen from the clip holding up her hair behind her ear. 'I moved to London almost six years ago for... well, with someone. But it didn't work out.'

Bingo.

'Forgive me, I know we've just met, but any man who walked away from you must be crazy.'

She raises a brow and sips from her takeout coffee cup. 'You assume it was a man.'

I feel my eyes narrow, playing along, but I know she's toying with me. She's sending pheromones all through my body.

She laughs before I have to respond. 'Okay, it was a man. An arsehole, actually.'

'There are a number of strains within our species.'

She smiles. 'And which strain are you?'

I'm about to answer when my cell phone rings. 'Sorry, I need to...' I lift the phone from my pocket to find Drew's face lighting up the screen. 'Drew, what's up?' I say, the words grinding through my teeth. *Cock blocker.*

The MILF, whose name I didn't even get to, holds up a hand and leaves with a smile. 'Master of time as ever, big bro.'

'It's like two-thirty in the afternoon over there. What can I possibly have interrupted?'

'Nothing, now.' I finally stuff my salmon in my mouth. 'What's going on?'

'Are you talking with your mouth full? That's bad manners, dude. Aren't the Brits teaching you anything?'

'Hey, your British girlfriend hasn't stopped you from calling when I'm in the middle of putting the moves on someone.'

'Ah, that's why you're snapping. Listen, I'm calling to say I'm looking forward to next week. I can't wait to see you, buddy.'

'Me too. I'm keen to see this new pad of yours in the Hamptons.'

'Right. So, I want to give you a heads-up. It turns out Emily is going to be in the Hamptons next week too. She's staying with her parents for their wedding anniversary.'

My stomach sinks so fast, that cherished piece of salmon might make a reappearance.

'Emily?' I don't know why I repeat her name. I heard it well enough. I clear my throat and lower my decibels. 'Great.'

Emily. My Emily. At least she was. She was mine at lower school, middle school, high school and college, until she wasn't mine any more. We were best friends, stuck together like a burger and cheese, a donut and frosting.

'Jake? You there?'

'Yeah, bad signal. I'm here.'

'You're still coming though, right?'

There's no way I won't bump into her if I go to the Hamptons. Not when I know her parents live right next door to Drew's new pad. In fact, it was her dad who told Drew the place was coming up for sale before it even went on the market. Emily's dad is an attorney, like Drew. He retrained after leaving the forces. I think he and Drew cross paths on the circuit from time to time. And our families know each other well; we spent years living on the same street.

'Ah, yeah, I'll be there.' I say the words with more conviction than I feel. 'Why would Emily being around change anything?'

Is she still with the dick I once called a friend?

'Oh, I don't know, Jake. Maybe because you guys were inseparable practically from birth, then three years ago you took a job in London when you could have worked for any hedge fund in Manhattan. Oh, and that's right, you haven't spoken to her since.'

'You don't know that I haven't spoken to her. And for your information, I always wanted to move to London.'

'Jake, you never wanted to move to London. Why would anyone move from Manhattan to London? Look, I don't know what happened between the two of you; I just wanted to forewarn you.'

'Well, consider me forewarned.' All that happened was one night.

One night was all it took to change everything, to obliterate years of friendship.

'So, I'll see you next week?'

'Yes, fine. Christ, are you going senile?'

'You're such a dick. I make allowances for you because you were an accident.'

Any other time, I might laugh. 'Jackass.'

'Yeah, but I'm a jackass who loves you, kid.'

'Yeah, love you too.'

We hang up and I stare at the half-eaten bowl of salad in my hand, then throw it in the nearest trash can and leave the park.

FFS.

* * *

Jess isn't answering her cell when I finish work. It's still broad daylight. That's a perk of my job. When I've made enough money for the day, I can leave. Out on the sidewalk, I put on my shades, flick my jacket over my shoulder, and start walking home. I could do with stretching my legs after my workout this morning. More than that, I could use the headspace.

I've tried not to think about whether I miss Emily. I used to. When I first came to London, I was crushed sometimes by how much I wanted to speak to her, even just send her a text message. We'd gone from speaking every day and knowing every single tiny thing there was to know about each other – or so I thought – to nothing.

I'm going to the Hamptons. I have to. I want to. My brother and our friends are going to be there. A week of hanging together in one house is bound to be crazy fun. But I just can't see Emily. What are we supposed to do? Act like nothing happened, continue as we always were? Or wind up in some kind of awkward handshake-hug, neither one of us knowing how to speak to the other?

By the time I get back to the apartment, I feel like I've stewed enough. I'm hoping Jess is home. When she's writing for her regular column or doing her freelance fashion stuff, she usually works from cafés because she gets too distracted at home. That's the thing about Jess; she's always easily distracted. Well, except when we're...

Anyway, she mentioned that she was putting together some new clothing ideas today, which could mean sketching or sewing and pinning things. When she does the practical stuff, she tends to go to a studio she rents from a friend in Camden. So, chances are, she isn't home, but damn, I want her to be. She's pretty much the only person I feel like speaking with right now.

I open the door of the apartment and don't see her but can smell her. That might sound odd, but she has this distinct scent, like flowers and candy. Sweet and bubbly. Like her. I also hear her music, 'Nine to 5' by Dolly Parton, is playing through the iPod dock on the dining table. Then I see her mess. Fabric, pens, scissors, thread, sketch pads, all scattered around the rug in the living room.

She's a walking hot mess. But an outrageously loveable one.

I call out for her but when she doesn't answer, I go in search of her. I hear her talking and assume she's on the phone. Her bedroom door is ajar so I nudge it open to ask if she wants anything, maybe one of her funky loose-leaf teas from Spitalfields market. But I don't ask because she looks uncommonly stressed. She's pulling on her bottom lip, her cell phone pressed to her ear as she paces in front of her window.

'You know I hate to ask. It's just that one of the magazines hasn't paid up this month and the fashion show I did last week actually cost me money. I have most of the rent but I'm about a hundred short and it needs to be paid today.'

She's talking about the rent on the apartment. I know because it's on my to-do list for tonight: transfer money to landlord.

'Oh, really? No, I understand. No, really, don't worry. I'll figure something out. It's one month. I always pay on time. I'm sure it will be fine. The magazine said the money should be in my bank early next week. Thank you, anyway. Sorry to interrupt your mai tai.' She chuckles, her dimples showing beneath her high cheekbones. 'Okay, speak soon.'

I move quietly away from her door, then call out to her from my own bedroom. 'Hey, Jess!'

'Hey! I didn't realize you were home.'

'Just walked in. I'm going to grab a shower, then I'll be out.'

'Great. I'm going to make some tea. Sencha with orange and rose petals. Do you want some?'

'Sounds gross. I'm good, thanks.'

What I could really use is a natural disaster to stop Emily going to the Hamptons next week. Okay, I don't mean that. But maybe, I don't know, high winds or something. Nothing fatal.

I jump in the shower to remove the office grime and pull on a pair of sweatpants when I get out. I take my Mac from under my bed and load my internet banking. Jess said she was a hundred short. I add two hundred pounds to my usual rent contribution and log off.

In the living room, Jess is sitting among her mess, her legs crossed in offensively bright floral lounge pants. She looks content. Happier than she was when I arrived.

She beams when she looks up at me. 'How was your day?'

'A lot less messy than yours by the looks of it.'

She twists her face and presses the tip of her index finger to her button nose. It's a thing she does when she knows she's being cheeky. 'Sorry. I didn't feel like heading up to Camden today, what with the underground strike. I'm almost done with this piece, then I'll clean up.'

'Don't move it for me; I can watch TV around you.' I take a seat on the sofa behind her and lean back, my legs spread. 'Do you have chopsticks in your hair?' I ask, studying the way she has pinned her brown locks.

'Oh, yeah. I've never eaten with them or anything, though.' Her words are only just decipherable as she speaks with a pin in her mouth. 'There. Done.'

She stands and holds up a silk top. It has an Asian feel to it. Like a short kimono. It is red with pink, green and blue flowers embroidered down the sides. But she has added lace around the low V-neck so it finishes like a ruched turtleneck. Okay, my descriptions of chick clothes aren't the best, but you can imagine the kind of things she makes. Fusion. Victorian British meets geisha.

'I like it,' I tell her, non-committal because I know what comes next.

'What do you like about it?'

There it is.

'I like the colors. Red silk works for me. As does black lace, for the record.'

She picks up a sofa cushion and throws it at me but smiles as she does. 'Your mind is in the gutter.'

'Always.'

'You're such a fiend.'

As she's clearing up the living room, I turn off her music and switch on the TV, selecting *BBC World News*. 'What are you doing for dinner tonight?' I ask. 'Do you want to go out?'

'Mm, can't. I have aerial yoga tonight.'

'What on earth is aerial yoga?'

'It's yoga but you do it hanging from the ceiling.'

'Really?' I raise a brow. 'If you like hanging from the ceiling you should have told me. I'm happy to put some ropes and a sex swing in my bedroom.'

She narrows her eyes and comes to sit on the arm of the sofa next to me. 'All right, what's wrong?'

How does she do that? 'What are you talking about?'

She snatches the TV remote from my hand and turns it off, forcing me to look at her. 'What is our number one rule?'

I shrug, knowing the answer too well.

'Let me remind you. We have sex and talk about having sex when we're intoxicated only. You're breaking the rules to distract yourself and I'm asking you what you need distracting from?'

'How do you do that? How do you get inside my head like that?'

'There's no skill to it, Jake. You're as easy to read as a pre-school book.'

I draw in a breath through my nose and lean my head back across the sofa. 'You know I'm going to New York next week? Well, it turns out Emily is going too.'

'Emily? *The* Emily? The Emily who made you emotionally unavailable?'

'That's the one.'

'Wow. You're going to spend a week with her?'

'Not exactly. Her folks own the place next door to Drew's and she's going to be there.'

'Maybe you won't see her?'

'I'll see her. For sure.'

'Are you contemplating not going? Because I don't think you should let her stop you.'

'I've contemplated it, but I have to go. Plus, my flights are non-refundable. I just... Argh, what happens when I see her, huh? What if all those feelings come back? Hell, they're probably still there, just repressed.' I groan and cover my face with my hands. 'Things got so screwed up in my mind about her. I'm afraid I'll do something stupid.'

She brings her hands to her lap and nods slowly. 'Maybe it's a sign, Jake. I mean, it's not like you've dealt with your issues. She's there, you're there. Maybe it would be a good thing. See her. Deal with your shit.'

'You and your signs.'

She points a finger at me. 'Hey, how many times have my instincts been off?'

She has a point. I turn away, trying to think of just one occasion. Then the proverbial lightbulb comes on right over my head and I snap my attention to her.

She holds up a finger and steps off the sofa. 'No!'

'Jess. Come on.' I follow her into the kitchen and pin her against the cabinets. She turns in my arms. Her face is just inches from mine. 'Please come with me.'

'No. I am absolutely not getting mixed up in emotional drama. I've had enough emotional drama to last me a lifetime.'

I give her my best puppy-dog eyes. 'You would ditch your best friend in his time of need?'

'Don't look at me like that. I said no.'

I flutter my eyelids. 'Pretty please?'

She pushes my chest hard, forcing me away from her.

I lean back against the opposite counter and rest my hands by my sides on the work surface. 'Come on, Jess. Save me from myself. Isn't that why we have our pact? To stop us from doing silly shit with other people? It's just like that.'

'Do you want me to stop you from having sex with Emily or from falling back in love with her?'

'Either. Neither. Both.'

She growls and rolls her eyes but I know she'll do it. 'Could you put on a shirt if you're going to ask me for favors? It's not fair.'

I laugh. 'Look, you've always said you want to run around New York like Macaulay Culkin in *Home Alone* 2. What if I agree to do that with you? We'll go find the bird woman – or similar because she's probably dead now. We'll fit that in around the Hamptons.'

She chuckles but when she looks at me, her eyes are full. 'I have always wanted to do that.'

I nod. 'Is that a yes?'

Her smile disappears, as if she's remembered something. 'Actually, I'm sorry, Jake, but I can't afford it.'

'Babe, you don't honestly think I'd force you to do something like this for me and ask you to pay, do you? It's on me. Obviously. In exchange for your services.'

'You make me sound like a hooker.'

'And that gets me all hot under the collar.'

She laughs. 'If only you were wearing a collar.'

'Smartass. Is that a yes?'

She scowls. 'It's a reluctant yes.'

'I'll take it,' I say with a wink. 'Oh, hey, there's one more thing you could help me with.'

'What now?' She busies herself in the fridge.

'Dumbass that I am, I hit the wrong key and overpaid my rent earlier.'

She pauses, holding a jug of water mid-air, her back to me.

'Yeah, I overpaid by like two hundred bucks. Think you could let me pay two extra and you pay two extra next month?'

She takes me by surprise when she puts down the water jug and steps into me, planting her lips on mine. It's a lingering kiss that gives me time to enjoy the softness of her skin against mine. I'm about to run my hands up her back and tell her to stick our intoxication rule when she steps back and looks at her toes, her cheeks flushed.

'Sorry. I… Thank you, Jake. Thank you for not making me ask.'

I lift her chin with my index finger. 'I have no idea what you're talking about.'

One side of her lips curls up. 'Okay, well, thank you anyway. I appreciate it more than you know.'

The apartment door flies open and Alex walks in, pulling his tie from around his neck. 'Fucking shit show at the office today. I hate my fucking job.' He comes into the kitchen and takes a bottle of beer from the fridge. 'Fuck my life. That's all I'm fucking saying.' He leans back against the kitchen counter. 'You two all right?'

Jess and I look at each other and laugh. Life would be a damn sight less colorful without our shit-for-brains housemate.

4

JESS

I guess we're going to New York. I don't like the fact Jake will be paying, but I'm not complaining about going. I mean, sure, I don't want to be caught up in his melodrama – Jake can be a little dramatic – but I would never have refused to go with him. Not for long, anyway. He would have ground me down eventually. I'm incapable of saying no to him. Maybe it's that charm of his. Perhaps it's the fact he made me remember how to smile again. Or it could be that he's the best man I have ever known. Well, with the exception of my parents. And right there is the biggest reason I had to say yes. My dad.

I don't remember much about my dad. I'm grateful to my mum that she shielded her nine-year-old daughter from the darkest days as much as she could. She tried to ease my heartache. I don't blame her for not being able to, for the fact my heart is still broken now, when I'm thirty years old, or that I wake up each day and think about him, and her. That my heart will never be truly whole. She was my protector, my armor. But I still saw some things that I can never forget.

I remember standing in the doorway of my parents' bedroom as my mum bathed the sores on my dad's arms and legs that developed as a result of his being bed-bound for weeks.

I can still see the fluorescence of the hospital lights, illuminating the cold corridors, through the gray of day, and the dark of night, because nothing was bright any more. The smell of cheap food, mingled with what I now believe was death, comes to me sometimes, as if I'm right there.

Sometimes, when I dream, I am back in his hospital room, watching as his organs failed and he slowly began to drown in his own mucus, only to be pulled back to life by nurses draining his lungs. I still remember holding my own breath as I watched him, feeling like I was sliding under water. It hits me when I least expect it, like when I'm watching a game of rugby and the players pile into a tackle. I can feel the fight for air of the player on the bottom of the pile. In those moments, I am nine years old. And I am helpless.

When I'm alone, if I don't stay busy, I have moments between conscious thoughts when I hear the last words my parents spoke to each other. They come to me clearly, as if my parents are right beside me, saying the words in real time.

My mum bent over his naked torso, which was not frail and skinny like you might expect in a man who had spent months fighting disease. He was large and bloated from the lethal cocktail of pain medication and steroids being pumped through his veins.

'You can't leave me.' My mum's voice broke and she began to sob. 'I don't know how to be here without you.'

My dad opened his eyes, unrelenting, even at the bitter end. For long seconds, I recall only hearing the ominous beeps of machines, counting down, counting him out of this world. Nurses shuffled in the corridor behind me and someone closed the door to give us privacy.

Eventually, my dad found his breath. He told her, 'You need to look after Jess. You promised me. As long as you have her, you have me.'

'No. I can't. I can't do it without you.'

She cried the words, as if she was oblivious to my presence in the room. I remember how the ground shifted beneath my feet as my dad dragged air into his lungs for the last time and almost sighed it out. As if he were resigned to letting death take him. As if he were relieved to be going to a better place. As if he were at peace.

What struck me then and has always stayed with me, is how a calm settled over me as I watched the pain and grayness leave my dad's face, as if it were draining from him as his soul left his broken body. Around me, nurses moved to take wires from his arms and end the one long, continuous bleep of the machine that no longer showed a beat but one flat line of color. His still heart.

A lady who had been supporting my mum in the recent days caught her and held her up, lifting her arms from my dad's lifeless body.

I remember distinctly that I just watched, keeping my eyes open when they wanted to close. I didn't cry. Not because I didn't understand that I would never see my dad in the same way again, but because I got the sense that he was still with me. He was in the room. His words, his heart, his soul still existed, just on another plane.

In the months after he died, my mum yearned for him desperately. She cried herself to sleep, his name on her lips and his photograph in her hands.

We were inseparable for eighteen months after that. Mum tried to keep her promise to stay on Earth for me. But even as I turned ten, then eleven, I could sense how much she wanted to be with him.

We always talked about him. We talked about the time he built me a trampoline in the garden and broke his arm being the first person to try it out for safety. We would smile about the breakfast pancakes he used to make with smiley blueberry faces. He didn't want his pancakes to be like everyone else's pancakes. He cooked the smile into the batter so my pancakes were actually smiling at me as I ate them. I often thought about the hours we spent watching movies at Christmas and how Dad promised that one day, we would go to New York and run the path Macaulay Culkin ran to get away from the Wet Bandits, from the toy shop, down Fifth Avenue and through a hotel. How he said we could one day go to Central Park in search of the bird woman. His time came to an end before we ever made it. But I'll do it for us both.

I smile at the thought of Jake running with me. I think my dad would have liked him. He would have thought he was a cheeky little swine, for sure, but a loveable rogue, just like I do.

When Mum got sick after my dad died, eighteen months to the day, people used words and phrases like *awful coincidence* and *tragedy*. I understood why people might think that but I knew, somehow, on some level, my mum had wanted so desperately to be with my dad, she'd willed her illness, made a deal with the Devil to see my dad again.

I'm not an idiot. I appreciate how crazy that might sound. But the thing is, you didn't know my parents. You didn't see and feel how much they loved each other. It was tangible. Like a presence in the room whenever they were together. It wasn't just the looks, the touches, the kisses my dad planted on my mum's cheek every time he left the house, or the way my mum smiled unconsciously when she was watching my dad do nothing but just be.

He was her soulmate.

They shared the kind of love people lie awake at night and dream of experiencing. Their bond was unbreakable.

My mum cried on her death bed, told me she had failed him. That she had broken her promise to look after me. But I said, 'He won't care, Mum. He'll be so happy to have you back. Sometimes, we break promises. We do and say things that hurt each other. But we only make real promises and only have the ability to hurt when it's someone we really care about. He won't care because you're with him. You're leaving me to be with him every day.'

She tried to raise her hand from her bed and reach out to me but she couldn't. The end was too close. I took hold of her hand and stroked her bare head, which had once been covered in long dark hair, like my own. And I said, 'You were broken, Mum. You've been broken for too long. Go to him now. Let him fix you.'

A silent tear rolled down her cheek. 'You are so brave and beautiful. I'm proud of you, Jessica.'

I squeezed her hand and sat by her bedside until she fell asleep. My dad's name was the last thing to leave her, as a whisper.

I knew then that she was going. She could see him and she was leaving me to go to him.

Those were the last words my mum ever spoke to me and his name was the very last thing she said.

I cried when she died. I cried because I longed to have both my parents back. Because by the time Mum died, I was only thirteen years old and I had to live with an aunt and uncle I'd hardly ever met. But I knew then and I know now, some things are bigger than you, or me, or this world. Some things have to be and will be and will last forever. Some things are more powerful than heaven and earth. Some things are timeless and will forever live on, in some form.

That's the love my parents shared and I am thankful every day that I got to see and be part of a love like theirs.

It is the greatest love I have or will ever know. I keep it alive, in my heart, and in my soul.

But I fear it. I fear its strength and the things that have to happen for it to live on.

I cherish it and I cower from it. Love is dangerous.

It has the ability to consume you. It has the power to end you.

And that's why the arrangement Jake and I have works just fine.

5

JAKE

'Jess, come on. We have to get to the airport.'

I'm sitting on the sofa in the living room with my packed case beside me, ready to go. Where, incidentally, I have been sitting for the last twenty minutes... ready to go.

'I'm here. I'm here.'

She comes into view, dragging her case along the corridor. She has on the most outrageously bright lounge pants I've ever seen, although she's paired them with a slouchy beige sweater and a thin scarf – for decoration, not because it's going to be too cold out. It is only 9 a.m. but the end of summer heat is keeping back London's chill.

She stops in front of me and holds her hands out from her sides.

'Mm, you're a five,' I say. 'You know I like that sweater. It's soft, practical and sexy as sin when it falls off your shoulder.' I wiggle an eyebrow. 'But those pants are horrendous.'

She laughs and resumes her hold on her suitcase. I move in and pick it up, handing her my hand luggage bag in return.

Our cab makes good time to the airport. I listen to Jess moan about how it would have been much cheaper to take the underground but as I told her: first, I couldn't be bothered with the hassle; second, it's quicker in a cab at this time in the morning; and third, it's my money and I'll spend it how I like.

By the time we get through security, I'm ravenous. I'm a big guy and I work out hard. Plus, I was brought up to have a healthy appetite. 'You won't grow big and strong on water,' Mom would say when we were kids.

I think some of it is her southern upbringing. My grandparents were originally from Tennessee. Mom likes fried food, especially fried peanut butter sandwiches. Killer, in more than one sense!

But I'm definitely not getting food right now. Instead, I'm following Jess around the duty-free store, 'window-shopping'. I've already picked up some gifts to take with us: tea, Harrods biscuits, the usual touristy stuff.

'Jess, please. You're killing me. You've sampled every moisturizer in here. You've sprayed yourself with a thousand perfumes, which are going to drive me nuts sitting next to you on the plane by the way. Can we get breakfast?'

She turns from the shelf of Union Jack souvenirs she's in front of. She has on enormous Union Jack glasses. She hits something on the arm and red LED lights start to flash as the glasses sing out the national anthem.

'Is somebody getting hangry?' she asks, planting her hands on her hips.

Despite being hangry, I laugh. 'You're such a goof. Feed me! Now.'

She puts the glasses down. 'One more minute. I want to look at—'

I pick her up over my shoulder and casually walk out of the store as she squeals, hitting the ass pockets of my jeans. I think she shouts, 'Put me down.' But it comes out like, 'Pu. Pe. Put. E. E. Eee. Down.'

We draw the attention of fellow travelers but I don't set her back on her feet until we're outside a restaurant that looks like it will give me a hearty breakfast.

I don't come up for air until my plate of bacon, sausage and eggs has been devoured.

'God, I feel better for that,' I say, leaning back against the booth.

She puts down her coffee cup. 'I'm pleased you do. I threw up in my mouth over here watching that.'

'Are you really only having a slice of buttered toast and a latte?' I ask. The vegan thing lasted less than forty-eight hours, in case you were wondering.

'Yep. I love airplane food. All the added salt and sugar they put in there to counteract the altitude taste-bud breakdown. It's the best.'

'Huh?'

'You've never heard that? Altitude, it effects your mind and body. You feel emotions more and you can't taste as well, so they put extra salt and sugar in the food.'

'Well, thanks, Doctor Jessica, for that insight.'

She smiles at me over her coffee cup. That sweet smile she doesn't often give. It's different from her playful smile, which is wide and open mouthed. And it's different from her fake smile, which is even wider but tight-lipped. This one, it stretches her lips but mostly shows in her eyes. Her eyelids widen a touch and her irises seem to sparkle like diamonds: chocolate diamonds.

When we first met, she hardly ever smiled. I still feel like each one is a prize, despite getting them often these days.

'So, what's the plan of attack when we get to the Hamptons?'

'Plan of attack?'

'Yes. I mean, are we trying to avoid Emily? Are we trying to rekindle a friendship with her? Are we like, "Hey, Em, I know it's been three years but let's bonk"?'

'*Bonk*? Are we back at school? And what was that voice? Was that supposed to be an impression of me or Terminator?'

She laughs. 'It was you and stop avoiding the question.'

The plan of attack. What is my plan of attack? How do I want this to pan out?

I have no idea.

'Are you two okay? Can I get you anything else?' Saved by the bell – or waitress.

'Just the check,' I say.

I'm still thinking about the plan as I pay the bill, as we board the plane and as we soar into the clouds. Maybe all I want is to come away from this week unscathed. Without having made a fool of myself, without having tried to rekindle something that never was between Emily and me, without being hurt. Maybe all I need to do is avoid her. Focus on my friends and family. Be civil if our paths do cross.

The problem is, I miss her. There. Happy? I've said it. I've admitted it. I miss the girl I grew up with and the girl who broke my heart.

'Hey, what are you thinking?' Jess asks from the seat next to me. We have a row of three to ourselves, yet we've decided to sit next to each other anyway. Jess in the window, me in the middle.

She's looking at me through concerned eyes. Her legs are tucked up on the seat, her arms wrapped around her knees. That she's small enough to do that, get comfortable in economy on an airplane, makes me a bit envious. My long legs are trying to stretch out under the seat in front but my knees are touching the pouch that holds the sick bag.

'Just wondering which movie to watch.'

She narrows her eyes in a way that says, *I'm letting this one go but you're not fooling me, dude.*

She springs forward excitedly. 'I know. We should pick a movie we both want to watch and start it at the exact same moment. Then we can watch together.' She starts to navigate the TV touchscreen.

I have to smile. 'Anyone would think you're thirteen, not thirty.'

'Be quiet. It will be fun. Come on, what do you want to watch?'

After a lot of scrolling and bickering, we settle on *Fences*, with Denzel Washington. Such a good actor! About that, Jess and I agree emphatically.

We both sit upright, braced to hit play. I count us in. 'On three. Ready? One. Two. Three.'

For some reason, we find it hilarious when we hit play and start our movies at the same time. I lift the arm rests either side of me, knowing from the three short breaks we've taken together – skiing in France with friends last year, Barcelona just the two of us because we both wanted to visit, Chicago, when she came along for the ride on one of my work trips – that she'll want to put her feet over me.

Sure enough, as soon as I have given her the green light, those dreadful lounge pants are across my legs and her feet are resting in the spare seat. Out of habit, I rub her legs as we watch the movie together.

As much as I enjoy *Fences*, it isn't enough to stop my mind wandering to Emily. To the sweet blonde I always looked out for. Who was by my side almost every day from age one year to twenty-four, whether I wanted her there are not. Annoying, beautiful, funny, sweet Emily.

That's why I find it hard to reconcile those memories with the last time I saw her. She was on her back, naked, her legs wrapped around the guy I thought was my buddy.

How could they have done that to me?

'Would you like chicken casserole or spinach pasta?'

I raise my head to the air steward and his big grin. 'Two chicken for us, thanks.'

As I answer, knowing she would have chosen the chicken over soggy pasta, Jess sits up and lets down both our food tables. The steward passes our food and sets about getting us each a small bottle of red wine. As he moves on, I put my chocolate mousse brownie dessert on Jess's tray. She puts her bread roll and cream cheese on mine. I'm not a huge dessert guy and she thinks uncooked cheese leaves the taste of cow leather in her mouth.

We eat in silence, watching the movie. The only thing Jess says is, 'She is breaking my heart. I'm going to start weeping into my chicken here.'

She's such a softie. For all her brassy exterior and the loud clothes, she's got a huge, mushy heart. And believe me when I say, it is always in the right place. She's honestly the best person I know. She's not too nice – you know, the sickening kind of nice – but if she likes a person, she'll do everything and anything for them. I know how hard her life has been, and God, I wish she'd never been dealt a shitty hand, or that I could have been there for her. But if her past has made her who she is today – wise, funny, empathetic – at least something good came of it.

'I'm stuffed to nuts,' she says, setting her empty wineglass down on her food tray.

'I don't get that. I mean, how stuffed are nuts?'

'Must you call me out on every expression I use?'

'No, I'm simply pointing out that it doesn't make sense. Why would you say something that doesn't make sense?'

She turns her lips to a pout and reaches out to my face, squeezing my cheeks between her fingers until my lips press together and I imagine I look like a fish.

'Is this a good look for me?' I ask.

'Mm, you're like a two.'

We're both laughing as our food trays are cleared. Jess leans her head against my shoulder and starts watching *Fences* on my screen.

I rest my cheek against her head and breathe in her familiar scent: a sweetness I can't describe, except to say, if I could bottle it, I would call it *Just Jess*.

We sit this way to the end of the movie and watch two more before we land. The exit through JFK runs smoothly, and we end up sitting in the car Drew has arranged for us right on time.

'I'm so excited to be in New York,' Jess says, looking out of the window like a kid: wide-eyed, jaw loose. 'Considering all the places I've been, it's kind of crazy that I haven't been here yet.'

As I watch her, a sense of calm settles over me. I'm home. With Jess. Putting aside the reason I've dragged her along with me, life is A-okay at the moment.

After an hour of making small talk with the driver, while Jess has had her nose almost pinned to the window, we're well on our way to the Hamptons. I've spoken to Drew to let him know we'll be on time for dinner. I'm looking forward to seeing his new place. I'm proud of him. We came from not much at all and now he's a named partner in a law firm, Statham Harrington, he has a great girl – she's a Brit but we won't count that against her – and now he has a pad in the goddamn Hamptons.

I realize I'm wearing a happy-goofy look when I notice Jess smiling at me. 'Are you excited to see Drew?'

'All of them.'

'Okay, remind me. Drew. Obviously, your brother. And he's with Becky, who I've spoken to on Skype. He's a lawyer, she's a patisserie chef. Then there's...?'

'Brooks. He's been Drew's best friend since they were kids. By default, he's one of my best friends. He owns Brooks Adams gym, which is huge in the city. He's with Izzy, the girl from Chelsea. She's a fitness and nutritionist-cum-dancer, musician type.'

'Got it.'

'Then there's Kit and Madge. Husband and wife. They have two kids, although I've no idea whether they'll be there. Kit roomed with Drew in college and Madge got with Kit around that time. I think Edmond and his wife Amelie are going to try to make it at some point.'

'Edmond, as in the celebrity chef who owns the restaurant Becky works in?'

'Exactly. And Marty, who is the Statham half of my brother's firm. They were both associates at the firm and at some point stopped competing against each other long enough to become good buddies and take over the firm together. And last, but definitely not least, is Sarah. Technically, she's Drew's legal secretary but I've only ever known her as an awesome woman and friend.'

'Drew and Becky. Brooks and Izzy. Edmond and Amelie. Kit and Madge. Marty and Sarah.'

'Yes, but not Marty and Sarah as in salt and pepper. Those two are single.'

She furrows her brow. 'Who's to say salt and pepper aren't single?'

I lean my head back and roll my eyes. 'Ah, remind me why I'm spending a week with you?'

'Because you love me and because I'm saving your arse.'

6

JAKE

The sun is starting to set as we pull up to my brother's new place. When I go to pay the driver, he tells me Drew has already settled the fare. He's always doing stuff like that. His old habit of never letting me pay my way will die hard.

I help the driver unload our luggage and then stand beside Jess on the quiet street, staring at the enormous white house in front of us.

'Is your brother royalty or something?' Jess asks.

'Yes. And I'm a prince.'

She glances to me. 'Now I know you're lying.'

There are four houses on the street, all facing the ocean. All big seaside properties. The gardens are pristine. Even the trees have been perfectly shaped. The grass is lush green.

Before I can say to Jess, *Let's head inside*, the door opens and a tall brunette bounds out onto the porch. 'Jakey!'

Sarah runs down the pathway and crashes into me, squeezing me tight. 'You must be Jess. It's great to meet you. Jake talks about you whenever I speak with him.'

That's one of those statements that would be awkward if Jess were a new girlfriend and I was playing it cool. But she isn't. And I do talk about her all the time because she's a big part of my life.

'Jess, meet Sarah. Sarah, Jess.'

'I love those pants,' Sarah tells Jess, making me roll my eyes and Jess stick out her tongue in a *ner-ner-ner-ner-ner* fashion.

I mouth to her, *Child*. And she mouths back, *Cock*.

'Jake, my man!' Brooks heads toward us in dark jeans and a white T-shirt that shows his inked arms and ripped muscles. He pulls me into a man-hug and thumps my back, then kisses Jess on the cheek. I wait for Jess to fall apart, like she has a tendency to do around ripped guys, but she gets through the meet in good shape. And, yeah, I'm comfortable enough in my own manhood to admit Brooks is like a real life, inked and more muscular, version of McSteamy from *Grey's Anatomy*. All women want him and men really do want to be him.

Brooks pulls the blond – who I know is Izzy because I've seen her commercials for dance and fitness on TV – under his arm. 'Guys, this is Izzy. She's crazy and annoying as hell but you'll come to love her.'

Izzy scowls, then laughs and gives Brooks an elbow to his ribs, which he deserves.

I lean in to kiss her cheek, then she starts practically singing something complimentary about those goddamn horrendous pants Jess is wearing. I take this as a good time to carry our luggage into the house.

Brooks helps me get everything inside when Drew calls out. As I enter, in search of his voice, I take in the bright, clean feel of the place. The light, wood floors, cream, fur rugs, white walls and nautical things hanging on the walls all scream money and beach. It's nice with a capital N. As I look up to the high ceilings and the spiral wood staircase, I trip over my own feet, bursting forward into the kitchen.

'Yep, that's my kid brother. Always big on the dramatic entrance.'

'Shut the hell up,' I say, as I make quick strides into Drew's arms – in a manly way, obviously. 'How're you doing, kid?'

'Not as good as you,' I say, pulling back and gesturing around the open kitchen space. 'Look at all this. And look at that hot chick you've bagged,' I say, clocking Becky as she comes toward me holding a glass of red wine. Her cheeks blush. She never can take a compliment. It's sweet and endearing.

'Hi, Jake,' she says, letting me pull her into a hug. She's the kind of woman I would think was lovely anyway, but that she makes my brother so clearly happy gives her more points than she can imagine. 'I take it you had a hand in the décor here, Becky, because you're the only exception to my brother's lack of taste.'

She laughs as Drew throws a wine bottle cork at me, which I catch. The other women come into the kitchen; Sarah, Izzy and Jess already seem to be pals.

'Becky, we've got ourselves another Brit,' Izzy says, clapping her hands.

'We're working on a large-scale British invasion,' Becky says, giving Jess a hug. 'It's nice to finally meet you in person.'

I watch the introductions for a minute, enjoying how happy Jess seems, forgetting why she's here and just being damn pleased that she is. I love that it's not awkward. There's none of that feeling of introducing your girlfriend to your friends and family because it's just Jess. Easy company. Kind, slightly nuts Jess.

'Well, I'll be damned,' Drew says. 'I thought you two were just roommates.' I turn and come face-to-face with my brother. Brooks is standing by his side. They both have their arms folded across their chests, eyes mocking me.

I point to them both. 'No. Shut the hell up with the mind trickery. Both of you. She's here to stop me doing or saying anything stupid. That's all.'

Brooks raises a brow and Drew tells him, 'Emily is here. Her parents own the house next door.'

Brooks nods slowly and whistles. 'Ouch.'

I give them a *what-the-heck-would-you-know* look right before I'm saved by Kit and Madge coming into the kitchen.

'Hey, I thought I heard you, buddy.' After the obligatory introductions, Kit says, 'We were upstairs singing the kids to sleep. Yeah, there's no need to look at me like that. I know it sounds wacko but they can't sleep without us singing the "Biggle Wiggle Bear" song.'

I can't help but laugh. A couple of years ago, Kit and Madge wouldn't have been caught dead singing about wiggly bears. 'They're here then, the kids?'

'Christ, no,' Madge says, retrieving a glass of wine from the large kitchen island. 'This is much needed respite. We were singing to them through FaceTime.'

'Jess, what can I get you to drink?' Drew asks. 'We're grilling for dinner.'

'Oh, just a sec.' She heads over to her hand luggage and pulls out the two bottles of champagne we picked up in duty free. 'Jake and I brought these, as a thank you.'

'I don't think anyone will turn down champagne. Thanks, Jess. Why don't you head outside and catch the sunset? I'll fix you a drink.'

Actually, it's me that fixes the drinks. I hand everyone a glass of fizz from a bottle Drew already had chilling and, after being told there's nothing I can do to prep food for the grill, I head out to where Jess has wandered out on the deck. She's taken off her scarf, causing her sweater to fall off one shoulder. She's taken down her hair too, the long waves falling down her back. It blows in the sea breeze, making her look like a portrait as she watches the red-orange sun fall. I take a moment to just enjoy the view. The serenity of it. Her peacefulness. Her aunt and uncle would be proud. They travel the world searching for this kind of peace and the incredible woman they raised is the picture of it.

As if she senses me, she turns and I hand her a glass of champagne. 'It's beautiful out here.'

I clink her glass with mine and look out across the pool, to the beach and the gentle roll of the waves against the sand. 'It really is.'

'I thought there was supposed to be a party?' I recognize Marty's voice before I turn to see him, stowing his cell phone in the back pocket of his jeans. He was always my least favorite of the group but the way he runs his eyes all over Jess, he just fell to the bottom rung of the friendship ladder.

'Good to see you, Jake.'

'Yeah, you too.' *Keep your eyes to yourself, though.* 'This is Jess.'

He winks at her. Like, actually winks, as an introduction. Who does that?

Brooks must sense my hackles standing on end because he gives me a look from behind Marty that says, *Don't worry about him.*

'Would you two like me to show you to your room?' Becky asks, coming out to the deck.

I carry our bags as we follow her up the spiral staircase, along a whitewashed hallway, under a ceiling made of glass. The place is incredible.

Our room is last on the corridor. Becky holds the door open and we follow her inside, both noting the one double bed.

'The en suite is through there. We're sorry about the double bed. It hadn't occurred to me to furnish the rooms differently until about ten minutes ago.'

'Don't worry at all,' Jess says. 'Thank you for having us in your home.'

Becky blushes and tucks her hair behind her ear. 'Well, it's actually Drew's place, not mine.'

'Becky, if you think for one second he's not already thinking that what's yours is yours and his is yours and all that, you're very mistaken. I know my brother and I know he is 100 per cent, prime time in love with you.'

She giggles but seems nervous. 'Did you just quote Meg Ryan in *Top Gun*?'

'See, that's why you can be my sister.'

She laughs this time, genuinely. 'I'll leave you guys to it. If you need anything, give me a shout.'

I check out the bathroom and the huge shower. Hell, yeah, I' d like to get Jess in that. Right on cue, Jess clears her throat in the main room.

'Erm, what are we going to do about this? Take turns in the bed and the other take the floor?'

With my hands braced on either side of the bathroom door, I raise a brow. 'Jess, I've shared a bed with you more times than I can count.'

'Not sober, and not to actually sleep in. Both of those things are against our rules.'

I shrug. 'Fine. Are you freshening up or coming back down with me?'

'I'll freshen up. But that doesn't solve anything.'

'Sure it does. I'm going to pour you a second glass of bubbles. If you're not sober, we can share the bed. Problem solved.'

Before she can process my words, I stride out of the room toward the smell of the grill in the yard.

We're sitting around on rattan furniture on the deck above the pool. The sun has dropped and solar lights have turned on around the lawn, the pool and down the pathway to the beach. When Jess comes back downstairs, she's wearing a thin, hooded sweater and tight, red jeans. She'd look normal if it weren't for the bright floral Chucks she's wearing.

I stand and hand her the glass of bubbles I promised. 'I would have said you're a six but because of the Chucks, you're more four to five.'

'Are you kidding me?' Sarah asks. 'You're calling her a five? She's a ten.'

Jess laughs. 'Thanks, Sarah. Jake likes to keep me grounded, don't you?' She squeezes my cheeks between her fingers in that way she does. 'He hates my fashion sense.'

She releases me and I watch her take my seat with a cocky smirk. Shaking my head, I take my beer and head over to where Drew is grilling.

I lean back on the fencing and watch him turn steaks, the fat sizzling as it drips into the hot gas. The smell has my mouth watering.

'I thought Edmond was coming,' I say.

'He is. The restaurant is closed Sunday and Monday so he's coming out tomorrow with Amelie. Why do you think I'm grilling tonight? I'm not cooking in front of Chef tomorrow.'

'Keep cremating that steak and you will be an embarrassment.'

He points with his grill tool to the steak. 'You want one? Then be quiet.'

I take his advice, swigging my beer.

'So, what's going on with you and Jess? I thought you said you were just friends.'

I glance over at her, where she's laughing with Sarah and Madge. They're all in kinks, the kind that have tears running down Madge's cheeks. 'We *are* just friends.'

'Really?'

'Yes, really.'

'I'm your brother, Jake. I've seen the way you're looking at her. Something's changed.'

'No. I mean, not, you know, mentally.'

He whistles. 'Friends with benefits. Let me tell you from experience, Jake, the next step is putting a ring on it.'

There are a couple of things I want to discuss about that statement but I start with the most pressing. 'Just because you couldn't take the heat with Becky, big bro, doesn't mean I can't handle it. We're both adults. We're great friends. She's the best. Neither of us wants to be in a relationship. She's emotionally destroyed, and I'm... doesn't matter. We're off point. And the point is, we have a good time together, we live together and she's my best friend in London. I wouldn't do anything to jeopardize that.'

He holds out his hands. 'Hey, whatever you say. Just be careful.'

'Now,' I say, 'let's get back to that point about putting a ring on it.'

He whacks me in the ribs so hard, I fold forward. When I raise my head, I realize why. Becky hands a plate of corn on the cob to Drew. 'Can't you two be left alone for five minutes?'

When the after sting dies down, I straighten to full height. Kit comes over with three cold beers. We each take one and start talking NFL.

'My money's on Kansas City Chiefs,' Kit says.

'They're cocky though, man. That's how you get tripped up. If they...'

I don't hear the rest of Drew's comment because my full attention has been drawn to the wooden pathway leading from the next house over. It is illuminated, like Drew's, with solar lights, all the way down to the beach. It must be seventy yards away. It doesn't matter because I'd recognize the figure of the woman walking down to the water if she was two hundred yards away and only a silhouette. I'd recognize the way her hips move, the small, bouncing stride of her petite frame.

Emily.

I don't know why but my legs move me from the grill to the edge of the deck and I watch as she reaches the end of the walkway and pads, barefoot, to the water's edge. Her white, summer dress blows, like her long, blonde hair behind her. She looks out into the distance and wraps her arms around her waist.

I don't know how long I'm fixed on her before Brooks pats my shoulder and says, 'Grubs up, buddy.'

For some reason, I don't turn to the grill. I look for Jess and find her in the same seat, staring back at me. She mouths, *Emily?* I nod. And she asks silently, *You okay?* I nod again, unsure what exactly I'm feeling but damn pleased Jess is here.

After plating the meat, we head to the kitchen island and help ourselves to rice and Caesar salad that Becky has made. When we all take our seats out on the deck, we start talking about plans for tomorrow. Jess lifts the croutons from her salad and puts them on my plate. I trade her for my anchovies.

Once we've helped Sarah load the dirty dinner plates into the dishwasher, Jess and I agree we're beat. It's close to four in the morning on our London body clocks. We kiss and hug everyone, wishing them all sweet dreams, and we head upstairs. Jess's movements are sluggish, so I put my hands on the small of her back and encourage her up the stairs.

'You can shower first,' I tell her when we're in our bedroom.

She looks again between me and the bed. She bites her lip, gathers her toiletries and heads into the shower room, closing the door behind her. I pull off my T-shirt, sneakers and socks and lie back on the bed, my arms tucked behind my head. I'm thankful for the fact I know the moves the amazing naked body behind that door can make, because it's stopping my mind from wandering to Emily. That's a place I don't want to go.

Jess doesn't take as long as usual in the shower, perhaps because she's tired, maybe because she's thinking of me needing to go in there before we sleep too.

She opens the bathroom door, steam creeping into the bedroom as she peeps her head around the edge. 'I don't think I planned this very well,' she says sheepishly.

I bring myself up to sit. 'Planned what?'

'Mm, could you maybe turn away until I'm in bed?'

'Excuse me?'

'Jake, would you just...?'

'Fine, fine.' I face the window but as soon as I sneak a glance and see her short silk nightie – bright because it's Jess and trimmed in lace that barely covers her nipples because she thought she would be sleeping alone – I watch her like a left tackle watches his quarterback: I don't take my eyes off her.

'Jake!' she yells, as she dives beneath the sheets, throwing a pillow at me. I laugh.

'Come on. If you tell someone not to look, you know the first thing they're going to do is look.'

She points and tells me, 'Go shower in cold water, mister, right now.' But the slight curve of her lips betrays her amusement.

Once I'm showered and my teeth are cleaned, I make my way into the bedroom. Jess is already sleeping on one side of the bed. Her hair is fanned out on her pillows. Under the low glow of the bedside lamp, her skin looks soft and inviting.

I chuckle to myself when I see the spare blanket she has rolled and placed in a line down the middle of the bed.

Are you that tempted by me, Jessica Walters?

Since she's sleeping, and technically, we aren't breaking any rules because we have been drinking, I drop my towel over the chair at the bottom of the bed and don't bother covering up my member. I slide gently under the sheets, trying not to wake her, and remove the spare blanket. I turn out the lamp and roll onto my side.

'Don't go getting any funny ideas, Jake Harrington. That blanket was there for a reason. And I hope you have some clothes on.'

Smiling, I press a kiss to her bare shoulder. 'Night, babe.' Then roll onto my opposite side, my back to hers.

7

JAKE

I'm sitting at my desk. The sky is dark above London. The office is empty, lit only by low night lights. I'm feeling pretty damn good about the investments I've made today.

I lean back in my seat and put my hands behind my head, closing my eyes as I stretch out my chest.

'Hi, you.'

The sultry voice draws my attention. I open my eyes to the Angel of Sin standing on the threshold of my office. Her brown hair has volume, like it does when we go out. Her eyes are dark and smoky. Her lips are red.

I don't know how Jess got into my office but it's my dream, I can do what I want. She's wearing a black, sexy as hell, lace corset.

My heart is racing as I take in her garter belt, her stockings, the stiletto heels that are begging me to take her standing up.

'Get over here,' I tell her, forcing the words through my dry mouth. When she stands in front of me, I run my hands over the lingerie, down to the perfect globes of her ass.

Since it's my dream, it's my prerogative to make this happen on my desk. I encourage her onto the furniture...

'Jake. Jake. What on earth, Jake? Get that thing away from me.'

I open my eyes in time to be battered by a pillow.

'You promised no funny business!'

What the actual?

I close my eyes and press my knuckles into the corners of them, willing sexy, bodice-wearing Jess to come back.

'Oh my God, why are you naked? And why do you have a...? For God's sake. That thing was poking my back, you Neanderthal.'

I hear laughter that I know belongs to Brooks outside the bedroom door. 'You lost control of your popsicle there, Jakey?'

Despite myself, I laugh. 'Jess, I'm sorry. You wore silk to bed. I mean, come on, it's not like we've never...'

She throws another pillow at me. 'When we're drunk!' She climbs off the bed and storms into the bathroom. Then she opens the door and pops her head around the corner. 'And for the record, what number was I in your dream?'

Now I laugh hard. 'You were a ten, babe.'

'Then we know for sure it was a dream.' She slams the bathroom door.

* * *

I do remember that this was the plan agreed to last night: that Izzy would lead the girls through a salsa and yoga class, while the butch-manly men went out for a long run. As I'm tying my laces outside on the deck, I'm wondering why I supported the plan.

'You didn't tell me we are running seventeen bastard kilometers, Brooks,' Kit gripes.

Brooks holds his right heel to his ass cheek, stretching his quads. 'It'll do you good. You've been doing great in my PT sessions lately. You're ready for this, man.'

Kit is the least fit member of our group. Brooks agreed to give him free personal training sessions at his gym in the city – which are normally impossible to book and wildly expensive – if Kit would take at least three sessions a week. From what I hear, he's been doing the three sessions and sparring with Brooks and Drew in the ring too. He's lost, at a guess, twenty-five to thirty pounds. Hats off to the guy. But that isn't stopping his face from contorting like someone's got his nipples in a tightly wound vise right now.

'I take it you're not coming?' Drew calls to Marty, who is lying back on a deck chair by the pool, his cell glued to his ear. I guess both named partners of the firm can't be on vacation at the same time. Marty shakes his head but continues talking into the phone.

'What time does Edmond arrive?' I ask, following Brooks' lead to stretch out my calves.

'Around lunch, he thinks. All right, are we set?' Drew asks.

As we head into the kitchen, the girls are coming out to the deck, yoga mats in hand, all dressed in Lycra. I try not to stare as Drew grabs Becky by the waist and pulls her into him. It's damn hard to miss the grind of his hips against her, though, as he grips her by the nape, whispers something – I can only imagine – into her ear, then crashes his mouth against hers.

'It's a good thing you didn't bring the kids,' I say to Kit, nudging him with my elbow. 'That's far from PG.'

'Are we going for this torture run, or not?' Kit all but growls.

Drew winks at Becky when he lets her go. Brooks spanks Izzy across her firm ass as he passes. Am I the only person not getting any in this place?

Out on the street, I pull on my cap, part to catch sweat, part to shield my eyes from the clear skies and bright sun. Brooks sets his watch, and our pace, as we move off in a row. Brooks, Drew and I can manage eight-minute miles, easy. We can talk and run. And, damn, is there a lot to catch up on.

We start with Brooks and Izzy. When they finally got their shit together, Izzy moved from London to New York. She rented herself a studio apartment and got a gig with a theatre company as a singer-cum-dancer. She's been playing open mic nights too. She's a singer songwriter and, by all accounts, pretty mean on a guitar. Somehow around that, she's working on a new fitness and nutrition book, too.

Kit's kids are beginning to sleep through the night, which means he's starting to get some action. Other than that, those two aren't up to much new. Madge wants to go back to work full-time but they have daycare issues.

My brother – well, we all just bore witness to how insanely happy he is with Becky. I'm delighted for him. He's finally got everything he's worked so hard for and a great girl too. I tell him as much and get a punch in the arm in return. Well-meant, I'm sure.

By mile three, we're starting to lose Kit. He waves us on, so we keep on at our pace.

'There's genuinely nothing between you and Jess?' Brooks asks.

'No, man. I love her. I mean, what's not to love? She's funny, she's smart. She's quirky and sassy and...' I trail off.

'Not getting out of it that easy, Jakey. And?'

'Ah, screw it. She's gold in bed. I mean, not just... ah, I don't know. Let's leave it at that.'

I catch the way Brooks and Drew look at each other. I can guess what they're thinking and yeah, they're right. It's not just her moves; it's the way I feel about her that makes it so damn good. But, like I said, I adore Jess, so of course that makes sex with her different from some one-night lay who I've never met before.

'To summarize, then,' Brooks says. 'She's funny, quirky, sassy.'

'And smart,' Drew jumps in.

'Right, sorry. Funny, quirky, sassy and smart. She's clearly hot. And she's like gold in bed.'

'Why aren't you marrying this woman?' Drew asks.

I laugh at his exaggerated tone and the way I'm being tag teamed. 'We just don't feel like that about each other. She lost her parents when she was young and she's convinced what made her mom sick after her dad died was a broken heart. She doesn't want to put herself in that situation.'

'And you?' Brooks asks.

I shrug, then lift my T-shirt to my face and rub sweat from my eyes. 'There's no way in hell I'm going there again. We're friends. She's my... she's kind of my everything. We live together, hang out together all the time, keep each other on the straight and narrow, look out for each other. I'm not losing that. I've been there before and it hurts like a bitch.'

'Finally, we start getting to the truth of why you and Emily haven't spoken since you left college,' Drew says.

There are three kilometers left in our run. It's probably too soon to pick up the pace for finishing, but now seems like the perfect time. I knock up my speed and call back to Drew and Brooks, 'You coming?'

They catch up to me and we run hard for just over two clicks. Until we run right into the path of Emily. She's in tiny running shorts and a sports bra. She's wearing her pink Polo cap. One I bought her a few years back because she kept complaining about her hair blowing in her eyes when we were running together. She looks as fit and lean as ever. She runs at a good pace. A pace I know is around eight minutes forty-five per mile.

She has her earphones plugged in and I also know she'll be listening to Lady Antebellum.

As if she feels us coming up on her heels, she looks back across her shoulder. She smiles when she catches sight of Drew and Brooks. Then her eyes lock with mine and she stumbles over her feet, toppling forward, her hands preventing her from fully falling. I raise my chin to the guys, telling them to run on.

'Are you all right?'

She doesn't look straight up at me. She keeps her head down and seems to be taking deep breaths. Her ribs visibly expand under the skin of her back. She unhooks the buds from her ears and tucks them into the strap around her arm that holds her music.

She eventually stands, looking up at me, her big blue eyes wide. 'Jake.'

I exhale a short laugh. Not because I find the situation funny. I don't. At all. I've been trying to avoid coming face-to-face with Emily since I last saw her, when she was shagging Brandon. I've done everything in my power not to see her.

'Who else would I be?' I say.

She brushes off my attitude. She never did let me get away with being a dick. Although, in this case, I happen to think it's justifiable. 'My dad said he thought you might be here this week.'

Nothing about her has changed. The lines at the side of her lips are the same. The dimple in her chin that never goes and gets more pronounced when she smiles is there.

'Don't you have anything to say to me, Jake?'

I don't know. I'm not sure I can form words, and even if I could, I don't know what I would say. She looks the same. She looks like my Emily. The Emily I brought home from school every day. The Emily I taught to skateboard. The Emily who asked me to take her virginity because she was afraid to let anyone else be first. But how can that Emily be the same Emily who ripped my heart out?

I lift the peak of my cap and set it back on my head with a sigh. 'I don't know.'

She reaches up and shuffles the peak of my cap to the left, like she always used to do, right before she says, 'It's crooked.'

When she says the words, I feel my lips curve up the smallest amount. She brings her palm to my cheek. Her touch feels... normal.

'I've missed you, Jake.' The words leave her as a whisper that's almost lost in the sound of rustling of leaves in the trees around us. 'Walk back with me?'

I don't know why I say it but I do. 'Race you.'

We both sprint down the last click, panting and laughing by the time we stop outside her parents' summer home. She stands with her hands on her hips, catching her breath. I can feel her gaze trained on me. I'm not ready for her. Instead, I look at the house and say, 'This is nice.'

'It's new. Ish. They bought it a little over a year ago.'

'In times gone by, I would have known that without you having to tell me.'

'You used to know everything about me, Jake.'

I turn to her now, by my side. 'Not everything.'

'I messed up. I screwed up and I'm sorry. But how long are you going to hold it against me? Are you honestly willing to throw everything away? Twenty-odd years of friendship?'

I glare at her now. 'I didn't, Emily. I didn't.'

'I just said I'm sorry! I said it again, for the hundredth time. I'm sorry. But it's not like it was easy for me seeing you with girls night after night at college. I hated it!'

'He was one of my closest friends. He was my roommate. You were in my goddamn house!'

It feels good to yell at her, even if we are in the street and a woman walking by with a stroller is staring at us. It feels good and too long overdue. But when her anger wanes and her eyes fill, I can't keep it up. My red screen retracts and I pull her into my shoulder. She wraps her arms around me tightly. I rest my chin on her cap.

'Stop crying. You know I hate when you cry.'

'I can't help it,' she mumbles against me. 'You smell so bad, it's making my eyes water.'

I feel her shoulders shake and laugh with her. 'How did we end up here?' I ask, not sure whether I meant to say it aloud.

She pulls back from my hold. 'I think maybe we loved each other too much.' As I'm trying to fathom what in the hell that cryptic mess means, she asks, 'Can I see you, while you're here? Just... to talk. Catch up.'

Do I want that? I'm not sure but the pleading look on her face makes me say, 'The gang's here. I'm sure they'd like to see you. There are some new additions now. I think you'll like them. Come over for dinner if you like.'

Her smile is barely there but it is there. 'I'd like that.'

I head into Drew's house toward the kitchen, where I find two sets of inquisitive eyes on me. Drew and Brooks share the same expression.

'Don't ask,' I tell them.

I take the glass of water they've poured for me and hand one to Kit who's finally made his way home. We take them out back. The first thing I notice is Marty lying on the deck chair, still clothed as he was when we left but without a cell phone in his hand. His arms are behind his head and his attention is focused on the decking by the pool. Drew, Brooks, Kit and I stand in a row along the pool's edge, following Marty's gaze to the five bodies bent over into downward dog. Five asses are pressed high into the air as the girls adopt their yoga pose.

There's only one pair of cheeks I'm fixed on and that's the pair that were the source of my morning wood. I watch Jess transition into another move. I recognize the plank, then she lowers her chest to the mat and pushes up on her hands until the only other part of her body touching the mat is the tops of her feet. Her back is arched, her head back, her breasts pushed up. I know what that body can do. How she makes me feel. And it is not good when I'm wearing sweats.

I look along the row and I know that each one of us is having thoughts that belong in the gutter. Then something occurs to me and I shout over toward the pool. 'Who the hell are you looking at, Marty?'

He snaps his head toward us and grins. *Snide mother...*

'He can take his preying eyes off my girl, or I'll damn well make him,' I mumble.

'I thought you said you were just friends?' Drew asks.

I give him a look that says, *Mind your own business*. Because right now, I'm really confused about where friendship stops and exclusive relationship begins.

The girls finish up their workout, ruining our ogling fun. They talk among themselves as they head up toward the pool.

When they near us, I can see what's coming... because it's something I'd do myself.

Jess shouts, 'Three, two—'

Before she can push me into the pool, I grab her arms, taking her with me as we plunge into the water alongside Brooks and Izzy. Drew and Kit crash in solo. We come to the surface and take a deep breath. I grab Jess, pulling her toward me. She bends her knees. Is it to stop herself from wrapping her legs around me? I would have preferred that option.

'You think that's funny, do you?'

She nods, laughing as she bites her lip, wondering what my next move will be. I lift her quickly, propelling her out of the water so she goes under again, making a tremendous splash.

She's laughing harder this time as she pops up. She swims over to me and this time, she does wrap her legs around my waist. Her hair tie has fallen out and her hair sticks to the sides of her face. As she grips my hips with her thighs, I rub the wet locks from her face, tucking them behind her ears. Our eyes meet and, call me crazy, but I think there's something in the look we share. Something that says, *we haven't done the thing this week*. A challenge. Something compels me to trail my thumb down her soft, red lips. The lips that I know kiss me so well. And I know we're sober but I'm certain Jess inches forward.

Whatever this pull I'm feeling is, she's feeling it too.

Then she pushes up and with superhuman strength, dunks me beneath the water. I break the surface. Her legs kick as she treads water.

'You needed to cool off, mister.'

As did she, but I let that slide. 'Yeah, I needed that.'

I climb out of the pool and strip down to my boxer briefs. I know she checks me out as I do. She pulls off her wet T-shirt, leaving her in leggings and a sports bra. The tat of roses is on view along the bottom of her back. What most people don't know is that buried deep in the rose petals, are two words: *Mum* and *Dad*. I smile to myself. I love that I know things about her no one else does.

As we head into the kitchen, we find Drew pinning Becky to the kitchen island with his hips pressed to hers. He kisses her neck as she whispers something to him. 'Dude, seriously, I can't handle you two on an empty stomach.'

I see Drew smirk, right before he kisses Becky in the way I imagine most women want to be kissed.

In the bedroom, it's clear Jess thought that too. 'They're great together,' she tells me.

I can't help the smile that tugs on my lips. 'Yeah, they are.'

She slips out of her wet leggings and pads toward me in only her sports bra and panties. The good Lord himself would be giving me a slap on the back right now for the level of self-restraint I'm showing.

'Want to make a bet, my betting friend?'

I fold my arms across my chest. 'What's the bet?'

'I think your brother is going to propose to Becky this week.'

'You do?' I feel my lips widen.

She nods. 'He got all his friends together for a week. In a new house that has enough bedrooms to host a family. And he can't take his hands or eyes off her. He is 100 per cent smitten.'

'I agree with everything you said. But this is the only time I've seen my brother in a serious relationship in my whole life. And they've only been together for a matter of months. For that reason, I think you could be wrong.'

She shrugs. 'When you know, you know, right? Do you take the bet?'

'Stakes?'

'The usual. You lose, you make me breakfast naked. I lose... well, I won't. This is happening.'

I run a hand along my stubble-covered chin. This is basically a win, win. I lose the bet, my brother gets engaged. I win, Jess gets naked.

I hold out my hand. 'I'll shake on that, miss.'

'Deal.'

'Now, would you please remove that fine ass from this bedroom before I break all our rules and shag you senseless?'

Her eyes widen, then narrow and grow darker. Her lips part. Then she fakes a laugh and walks, a little unsteadily, to the bathroom.

Ah, Jesus, I really do need to have sex with her. This is the first week in – hell, ten weeks? – that I haven't had a fix of her body. It's the first time I've realized she's become a craving.

She closes the door and I hear the shower turn on. Then I stare at the closed door. My heart starts to beat faster in my chest. My breathing quickens. I really want a piece.

I know the rules. I know exactly why we put them in place. But hell, at this moment I'm struggling to think of one good reason why we can't break them this once.

I strip out of my boxer briefs and head into the bathroom. I pause, my hand on the door handle. Just once. What's the harm?

Something is telling me this is a bad idea. Something makes me pause. But I open the door. She turns to me. The hot shower has filled the room with steam but I see her beneath the multiple shower heads. Smokin' hot. Looking at me the way she looked at me moments ago. Those hooded eyes. The slight gap between her lips.

Like a wave, lust crashes over me and hurtles me toward her. I move into the shower, push her back to the tiled wall, and cover her mouth with my own. She groans as she kisses me back just as fiercely.

Words are coming to my mind and threatening to break from my lips. I want to tell her how much I adore her. How good my days are when they're filled with her. How no one has ever satisfied me like she does.

Holy shit!

I pull back from her and walk backward until my ass is pressed to the wall opposite her. I'm breathing harder now than I was after running earlier. I drag a hand through my hair.

Her eyes are closed, her head resting back against the tiles.

'This is why we have the rules,' she says.

I don't know whether to confirm that statement, or whether to linger on the fact she might have had similar thoughts to my own. Instead, I drag my hands over my face and leave the room without saying anything.

Downstairs, Sarah is stuffing bacon into rolls and making a mountain of food in the middle of the table. I boil the kettle and find one of the boxes of loose-leaf tea I picked up in the airport.

By the time I set the tea on the table, everyone else is seated except for Jess. For a moment, I worry we crossed a line. I don't want anything to be awkward between us. I couldn't stand it if that were to happen with Jess.

But she strolls into the kitchen, her bright print kaftan flowing as she walks. As outrageously bright as the sheer material is, she looks beautiful. Her hair wet. Her face makeup free. Her feet bare.

'Oh, Jess, I adore that outfit,' Sarah says.

'Thank you. It's actually from my summer collection.'

'You made that?' Madge asks.

My insides fill with pride as they talk about how skilled Jess is. I already know she is. Not that I blow smoke up her ass. That's not how we roll.

As I finish stirring her tea, I feel her hand on my back. 'Are we good?' she asks.

I wrap my arm around her and pull her to me, pressing my lips to her hair. 'We're good. Just a blip.'

She gives me a soft smile, then her eyes fall to the tea pot. 'Is that my funky tea?'

I chuckle. 'That's your funky tea.'

'Thanks.' She takes the pot and moves to the table.

'For the record, you're like a six. And that's only because I can see your bikini through that thing.'

She laughs as she sits and everything is right between us.

* * *

We're all lounging by the pool, reading, listening to music, dipping into the water, having a beer. It must be seventy-five to eighty, which is warm for this time of year. Maybe someone is smiling down on us.

I pull my knees up in my board shorts and bring my hands behind my head, knocking my cap forward enough to shield my eyes as I shamelessly watch Jess move from her lounger to where the music dock is on a table in the corner of the pool area. By magazine standards, she might be considered normal looking, whatever that means. She doesn't have legs that go up to her neck. She isn't six feet tall. She doesn't have blonde hair that's polished and perfectly straight and runs down to the small of her back. She's toned but she doesn't have abs or cut in at the hips. Her breasts aren't large; they're just perfectly sized for her body – and my hands. And the bones at her collarbone and sternum don't show through her skin. So, I can't tell you why I'm lying here with a semi-on and thinking she is an absolutely sublime human being. But damn it, she is. She's her own person. She looks her own way. Sounds her own way. Dresses her own way. And these days, she's confident. She's come out of her shell in so many ways since we first met.

I am one lucky man for getting to share bedtime her. That's what I'm thinking as Becky turns her head on the lounger next to mine and lowers her book to her chest.

'Jake, if you're trying to be inconspicuous, it isn't working.'

Cover blown, I readjust my cap.

Sarah sits up on the lounger to my other side and brings her legs over so she's facing Becky and me. 'To make sure I've got this. You two are best friends, right? I mean, you don't need to answer that because I can see how well you get along. You're like the other half of each other. But you're also sleeping together.'

'Only when we've had a drink,' I correct, 'and we don't do the sleep-over thing. Well, we were never supposed to.'

'Aha, right. So, you adore this woman. We love her, just so you know.' Becky nods too, as she comes to sit and join the tag team against me. 'And you're totally hot for her.'

I know where this is going. I look around for some moral support but none of the guys are paying attention to the three of us.

'Tell me again why you aren't together.'

I can feel myself getting defensive and my words coming out curter than I intend. 'Sarah, you know as well as anyone that men and women can be friends. Look at you and Drew.'

She raises her hands. 'Absolutely. The difference is, I've never slept with your brother. Nor have I ever wanted to sleep with him. No offense, Becks.'

Becky laughs. 'None taken.'

'Look, she doesn't want more and neither do I. Why would we ruin a good thing?'

Our attention is stolen by a burst of laughter from Jess. The three of us turn our heads to where she's standing by the speakers with Marty. His hand is resting on the small of her back as he leans across her shoulder, pointing to her iPhone, where I suspect she's scrolling through music.

Every muscle in my body tightens.

'That's why,' Sarah says. 'And don't roll your jaw at me, Jake Harrington.'

Groaning, I drop my head back on the lounger. Yeah, so I can't stand Marty, or any man, being near Jess, for that matter. That doesn't mean I'm ready to risk our friendship by changing things between us. Or putting myself out there just to be shot down by the guards she keeps armed and ready on the high walls she's been building around herself since she was nine years old.

'He needs to take his filthy hands off her.'

I know I've said that out loud when Sarah gets up from her lounger and heads over to Jess and Marty, faking a reason to get Marty's attention.

'She's so amazing,' Becky says, watching Sarah. 'I think she could turn me.'

I laugh. I hope Drew does propose; I'd like Becky to stick around.

On cue, Drew comes over, hands Becky a virgin mojito and slides onto the lounger behind her, pulling her back between his legs to rest on his chest.

'Jake, did Drew ever tell you how we got together?'

I narrow my eyes. 'Kind of.'

'Well, I bet he didn't tell you about his note and my mediocre desserts.'

'Ah, don't do this to me, Becky,' Drew grumbles.

'Sorry, baby, but I think it's for the greater good,' she says. 'Obviously, desserts are my thing. I'm a patisserie chef, after all. I gave Drew some sample desserts one night when he came to the restaurant. I was thanking him for buying me breakfast, which is another story, and because I was trying to convince him he could be a sweet man.' Drew rests his chin on Becky's head and tightens his hold around her. 'So, he took my desserts in a doggy bag. The next day, he came to the restaurant and left a note for me. Do you know what it said? It ranked my desserts out of ten. He gave them all five or six. Then at the end, he signed off with something like, "I'm still not a fan of mediocre desserts".'

'You're such a dick,' I tell him, as the three of us laugh. 'That's so uncool, man.'

'Jake, have you grasped the point of my story?' I feel my eyes narrow. 'Clothes are Jess's passion and every day, you basically call her mediocre.' There it is. The penny. Falling. 'You tease her. You flirt with her. But what you're actually telling her is the exact opposite. She looks good. You're proud of her. And the even bigger point is, you're just like your brother. All the five out of tens you give her now are going to lead to you two being together once you both get your shit together.'

Once we both get our shit together? Do we have shit to get together?

'You've been spending too much time with Sarah,' I say. 'I hear what you're saying, but Jess and I aren't like you and Drew. We're already friends, you know? I wouldn't give her up for the world. And I know too well how easy it is to mess up a good thing.'

With impeccable timing, a low voice comes from inside the house –
a mixed-up American accent with a French lilt, or maybe a French
accent with an American lilt. 'I have focaccia, brie, jambon, fine wine.'

Edmond steps onto the decking with his arms full of boxes. Amelie
appears at his side, holding two large, brown paper bags of food, a
baguette poking out the top of one.

8

JESS

Seeing Jake with his friends and family warms my heart. The way he cares for them is something I've admired in him since the first day we met. It's something I never had, and I'll admit it makes me a little envious. I've never had a network of people to love, and love me back, the way Jake has. And he's so easy around them. The way he is with me. He's himself with everyone. He doesn't play up to crowds. That charm, which is sometimes flirtatious, sometimes endearing, and sometimes a little goofy, is natural for him. He's a nice guy, a great guy. And, boy, he can make me laugh. For the last two years, he's continuously managed to find a smile in me that I didn't think I had.

It's not that I'm unsociable, or that I never *wanted* to be happy. I just wasn't. I like chatting to people and learning new things. I love that my travels have meant I've experienced so many cultures and walks of life. But I can't boast that I ever had friends. The closest I came to friends were ladies working in rice paddy fields who didn't speak my language, and Danny. He's the one exception. And that didn't end well.

I was fourteen years old when I arrived in Laos with my aunt and uncle.

'Look at the lush greenery. Smell that air.' Aunt Ruth sucked in a breath that made her nostrils flare.

As I breathed in with her, I got the distinct scent of fish and something foisty coming off Laos's Mekong River. I didn't get the freshness she was talking about at all.

I had to release my breath before my aunt. Her daily yoga and meditation meant she could inhale for an insanely long time before needing to release. Despite being forced to do yoga, tai chi, and meditation a lot over the last two years, I wasn't at her lung capacity. Not even close.

'I can sense the tantra is going to be wonderful here,' Uncle John said.

Aunt Ruth rocked into his side with a short giggle, which told me they weren't talking about Hindu and Buddhist traditions but tantric things between the two of them that I didn't need to know about. That I didn't want to know about.

As our large backpacks – basically containing the entire contents of our lives – were lifted off the barge and set down among a pile of other backpacks, we wormed our way between the gap-year students and found our luggage.

At this stage, despite the weight of it, I was a dab hand at swinging my backpack up from the ground and onto my back. Laos was the eighth country we'd moved to in the, more or less, two years I had been in the care of my aunt and uncle.

After Mum died and the funeral was done, we spent one week buying second-hand trek clothes and camping gear before we set off on our travels. During those years, I spent some time in formal education but mostly I was home-schooled by my aunt and uncle. My uncle was an ex-professor of history and classics, until he met my aunt and they found themselves in the Galapagos Islands.

As they traveled, my aunt and uncle picked up jobs here and there, teaching English and yoga. Working bars. But mostly they did that to 'give back' because they lived reasonably well – for nomads – on the small amount of rent their few properties brought in each month.

The sun was setting over the Mekong River as I looked back in the direction we had traveled. The humidity, together with being squished onto a barge with a load of other travelers for too long, had me feeling grotty. I wanted a shower but I didn't want to use a hand-held hose to trickle water over me as I sat on a toilet because the bathroom was too small for separates. I wanted to go home. At least, to the home I used to have with my mum and dad. I wanted to shower in my own bathroom and sleep in my own bed.

But I reminded myself, I didn't have a home any more. They were gone.

I hoisted my luggage higher on my back and tightened the padded straps across my shoulders. I nudged through the crowd of travelers with their *Lonely Planet* guides and set off up a hill with my aunt and uncle. After twenty minutes, we found the hostel we were spending the night in.

A petite Asian lady met us at the entrance of the single-story concrete structure, which looked like it had been painted white a long time ago. '*Sabaidi.*'

The three of us dipped our heads in reply, repeating her greeting. Ruth paid six dollars for a double room for her and Uncle John and four dollars for my bunk in the unisex dorm.

Even though I was younger than the gap-year students, they always smiled and said hello. The lone travelers always tried to talk more.

I found my bunk bed and took off my backpack. A girl, maybe nineteen or twenty, hung over the side of the top bunk and held out her hand. 'Hi, I'm Meredith.'

'I'm Jess.'

'Are you traveling alone?'

I shook my head. 'My aunt and uncle are staying in a private room.'

She chuckled. 'They've found tantric practice then?'

I rolled my eyes. 'God, don't joke. I can barely deal with their level of hippie. If I think about them sustaining sex for as long as they can, it might finish me off.'

We talked a little as I unpacked my washbag, my shorts and vest to sleep in, and some clothes for the next day, knowing we were moving on early. I didn't ask too many questions about her and I didn't bother telling her much about me. We spoke about the books we were reading and where in England we came from. There was little point establishing any kind of friendship.

After showering, I lay on my bunk and read, using my small flashlight once the dorm lights were turned out. When I finished the book – my tenth in the last three and a half weeks – I set it on the floor, where someone else would find it and make use of it when I was gone, and I went to the place I went every night. I went to find them.

I searched my memories for their smell, something that became harder each night. I tried to remember their voices, calm and loving. I willed myself to see every detail of their faces. My dad was becoming so distant, it terrified me. My mum came to me more easily, but she was fading too.

Silent tears rolled down my face and I could feel my heart beginning to beat too fast as I begged my mind to bring them back to me.

As my chest tightened, I heard my mum's words. *Deep breaths, baby. Deep breaths.*

As I took control of my lungs, I told them in my mind how much I loved them. How I would see them one day, and how I would never forget them.

Eventually, my inhalations became longer.

The next morning, my cheap pocket alarm went off at four thirty. I silenced it as quickly as I could, although I still received a few grumbles from travelers who'd stayed out late drinking and wanted to rise at a sensible time. When I made it outside the hostel, Ruth and John were already waiting for me. Aunt Ruth held out a bag of rambutan.

'Good morning, sunshine. Did you sleep well?'

I took the red prickly fruit and bit through the shell, then discarded it to suck the sweet translucent fruit inside. Nodding as I chewed, I eventually told her, 'Can a few hours qualify as sleep?'

She raised a brow. 'Were you reading again?'

That and they had forced me to wake at the crack of sparrows. I shrugged and took another rambutan from her as we headed in the direction of a local bus. We rode with chickens, local people carrying huge bags of rice, and the occasional baboon that jumped on the roof when we stopped. After my bum had gone numb from the hard seats and the bumpy ride over dirt roads and potholes, we arrived in Vang Vieng.

Once we'd dumped our backpacks in yet another hostel, Ruth and John prepared themselves for yoga and meditation. I was hungry and tired of sitting down, so I left them to it and went to explore the city.

You're probably thinking I was too young to be exploring a new place, in a new country, with a vastly different culture from the small country town in England where I had grown up. Frankly, I was. But I will say this for Ruth and John: they never treated me like a child. They always spoke to me as if I were a young adult. Sometimes, I did wish they would put an arm around me, nurture me, tell me it was okay to be a child. Other times, I realize, looking back, they showed me things about the world and people that I would have never experienced if I had stayed in my small town.

I wandered until I reached the river. There, I listened to the water as it rolled idly by, as if it didn't have a care in the world. As if it had nowhere to go, but that didn't matter because there was only one direction to travel. One path. And it would have to flow the course. It was the destiny the Earth had given it. It just had to get on with it. I felt the inevitable flow of the river in my own inability to control or change my path.

Then I picked up my head and gasped at the lush green mountains towering over me. I thought I had never seen anything more beautiful in my life. In that moment, I understood how small and inconsequential I was in the grand scheme of life and death. And I made a decision to accept that I couldn't change my destiny. It just was. I just was. I was alone and that had to be okay.

For two years, I had longed to have a sibling, or to stay in one place long enough to make a friend. I had pleaded with whatever higher power existed, I had begged my parents to send someone to me, someone who could share my pain and alleviate the weight in my chest, if only by an ounce.

Under the shadow of the mountains, I cried. My tears fell to the river's edge and I imagined them being carried away, taken to somewhere my parents could hear me. I knew that somewhere, one day, I wouldn't be alone. That one day, my flow would find a home, where it could be still. Until then, I had to protect myself. I had to look out for my heart. Because I knew it couldn't take any more pain.

Ruth told me that I should enjoy the freedom of traveling and not having a routine like other kids. She said I should see the branches of the tree she and John gave me. 'Feel the wind through your new leaves, Jess. Experience. Feel,' she would say. I decided watching that river flow to experience my branches and leaves. And I never gave up hope that I could someday have roots to my tree and that they would anchor me.

* * *

I was eating street food in Luang Prabang with Ruth and John, sitting on a pink plastic stool for children at an elderly gentleman's stall, a bowl of sticky rice in my lap, when I overheard some other travelers being told about the Buddhist Alms Giving Ceremony that took place each morning. When I enquired about it, the street vendor was happy to share his knowledge with me.

'Every day at sunrise,' he told me, in his broken English, 'the monks come from their temples. They bring baskets and people offer them food for their one meal of the day.'

'Could I go?' I asked him.

'Of course. All welcome. But you must obey rules. Cover your skin and arrive before the monks. Offer your food but do not get close and do not try to talk to them. You must be respectful.'

I nodded. 'Of course.' I turned to Ruth. 'Can we go?'

'We have meditation at sunrise, Jess. But you could go alone.'

Alone. Of course. It was something I was too familiar with.

But I bought rice from the street vendor and took it home that night. I asked Ruth and John to wake me before sunrise and I went down to the ceremony. I stood next to a local lady who barely spoke English, as we waited in a line along the street the monks would traverse. She tugged on my baggy pants and kaftan, which I wore to cover my knees and shoulders. She pointed to her feet, which were naked, and then to mine, which were in sandals.

Understanding her, I took off my shoes and followed her lead as she sat on the ground and tucked her legs beneath her. When the monks came by in a line, I, like her, held out my rice for them to take, sneaking a glance, even though I was told not to stare.

The young boy I offered food smiled at me, even though I knew he shouldn't, and I couldn't help smiling as I tucked my head down again.

The sun began to rise and heat my body. I felt the warmth of the new day and the warmth of being part of something. It kept my shadows away and it masked my pain, even from me, for the moments I sat on the ground. I promised myself I would hang on to the feeling for as long as I possibly could. Tomorrow, I could steal the heat of sunrise again.

After the ceremony, I wandered the street market. I bought a banana and a handful of rambutan for breakfast and I sat on a wall to eat, looking out to the Mekong River.

'I'll trade you mango for a rambutan?'

I looked up to see a young man, perhaps eighteen. He sat next to me on the wall and we traded fruit.

'Have you been to the giving ceremony?' I asked.

He nodded, sucking on his new food. 'These are good,' he said.

'They're my favorite.'

'Did you enjoy it?'

'The ceremony?' I asked. He nodded again, seemingly not a boy of too many words. 'Yes, I liked it very much.'

His eyes narrowed and he seemed to study me. 'What did you like about it?'

I couldn't tell him that I liked being among people, having something in common with those around me. So I shrugged. 'I like learning new things.'

He nodded again and looked out to the water, where the sun was now midway through the sky. 'You know, Buddhists believe in karma. It's one of their key beliefs.'

'Karma? You mean like what goes around comes around?'

'Sort of. It's more than that. Have you heard of The Four Noble Truths?'

I shook my head.

He spat the pip of his rambutan into the river, making my nose scrunch with distaste. 'In Buddhism, people believe that we cling to impermanent things. Because of that, we enter the cycle of painful death and rebirth and being unsatisfied between those two things. They call that state, being unable to satisfy oneself, *dukkha.*'

Dukkha. I repeated the word a number of times in my mind. 'I'm not sure I follow.'

'See, we are constantly trying to find happiness in impermanent things, therefore, we can never be truly happy.'

I would come to understand those words one day when he spoke them to me again. But it would not be that day. I was uncomfortable with my lack of knowledge. I knew on some level, those words were speaking to me, speaking to my soul, and that somehow, they were words I was supposed to hear in that moment.

So, I changed the subject. 'What are you? Some kind of eighty-year-old prophet trapped in a teenager's body with bright-green eyes?'

He smiled. It was a cute smile. It made him look younger but still a few years older than me.

'You're pretty,' he said. 'And I'm Daniel, or Danny.' I felt my cheeks blush red. I couldn't think of a time a boy had paid me a compliment.

I looked out to the river as I said, 'Well, Daniel or Danny, I'm Jess.'

We walked back to the market without talking much. I couldn't resist running my fingertips across all the fabrics – silk, cotton, satin, lace – in bright, bold colors. That would be the day that started my obsession with fashion designing, and it would be the start of my *self-made hippie wardrobe*, as Jake would call it. But it has more relevance now because it is part of the reason that Jake and I could never be together.

9

JAKE

I watch Jess as she rolls her hair into a bun and sticks it into place with two fancy-looking chopsticks. She turns to me, her hands held out from her sides. 'Well?'

She's wearing the Asian-style wrap top she made a couple of weeks ago, teamed with black, low-rise pants and her own bold print wedges. She looks unique, fantastic, and her all at once.

'Four. Sorry, babe, I'm not in an Asian mood.'

She rolls her eyes as she adds gold-leaf earrings. 'That's because you have your sights on all the French food Edmond and Amelie brought with them.'

When she turns her back on me, I notice one of her chopsticks isn't pushed quite far enough into her hair. I get off the bed and move behind her. She watches our reflection in the mirror as I slide the chopstick farther into her bun. 'Better.'

Reaching back and raising her hand to my jaw, she smiles softly. She squeals when I take her by surprise, biting her hand.

'I like this shirt on you,' she says, twisting to face me. She fiddles with the collar of my pink shirt. I breathe her in, the scent I love on her. She looks up to me, her teeth pressed into her lip. I would pay big money to know what is going on in her mind right now. I stare at the lips she's painted red. They look inviting. Too inviting. I tug her bottom lip from her teeth with my thumb.

'You have lipstick all over your teeth,' I lie.

'I do?' She starts rubbing her teeth frantically with her finger, breaking the dangerous tension. When I laugh, she gives me a thump in my pec. 'I hate you.'

'You love me.' I tuck her under my arm and we head downstairs.

The smell of beef bourguignon, or maybe coq au vin, hits my nose before we even make it to the kitchen. It could be either because I know Becky and Edmond decided to cook both dishes for everyone tonight. Whichever, it smells damn good. I tell Becky and Edmond as much as they work around each other, seamlessly navigating chopping boards, checking on food in the oven. I can see how these two work well together in the restaurant.

Edmond leans in to taste some kind of mixture Becky has in a large bowl. He takes a bit from the teaspoon she holds. 'More vanilla,' he says.

She nods. 'Agreed.'

'Those two are like a well-oiled machine. It's impressive,' I say, stepping onto the decking.

'I told them they didn't have to cook but they love it,' Drew says, handing Jess a glass of champagne and me a bottle of beer.

'You can't tell a chef to stop cooking,' Amelie says.

Everyone is sitting around on the wicker furniture. Jess is chatting with Madge and Izzy about style tips. I love that she can mix with everyone easily. It's always been one of the things I've admired about her. She can talk to anyone, in any setting. I guess many years immersed in different countries and cultures is the reason. But, right now, I wish she wasn't deep in conversation, because my mind is wandering to Emily and the fact she could turn up at any minute.

What was I thinking inviting her here tonight?

I don't have too long to panic because the flow of Emily's dress in the wind catches my eye as she comes up to the house from the beach. I watch her and exhale heavily, slowly. It's been more than three years we haven't spoken, and the last feelings I had for her were far more than friendly. I was contemplating spending the rest of my life with her. The girl I grew up with. The girl I loved. The person whose presence in my life meant as much as my parents', my brother's.

Jess breaks from her conversation to follow my gaze. She puts her hand on my thigh and squeezes. 'You've got this, Jake. You've got this.'

I nod, not sure that I've got this at all, but grateful for the sentiment.

Emily and I meet on the decking below the pool. She hands me a bottle of wine but keeps hold of the flowers she's carrying. Her skin is pale, her lips a light pink. She has a small amount of makeup around her eyes. Her hair is loose and blowing in the wind with her polka-dot dress.

'Hi,' she says, clearly as unsure as I am.

'You look nice.'

'Thanks.'

I lean in. I think to kiss her cheek, which is weird, because that's not our thing. She goes for a hug and we wind up in an awkward hug-kiss situation.

'This used to be easy,' she says with a short laugh.

'Did we ever hug and kiss?'

She bunches her lips together in a way I'm familiar with and shakes her head. 'Only that one time.' She winks and I chuckle. The heavy air diminishes.

'Come on up.' On the deck, I introduce her to Izzy and Becky, not needing to introduce her to everyone else she's already met.

Conveniently, Jess has disappeared.

'Ems, I haven't seen you for an age,' Brooks says. He pulls her into conversation, which gives me a chance to get myself together and look around for Jess. Eventually, she comes onto the deck.

'She's even more beautiful in real life,' she whispers to me.

I decide against responding to that. For years, I didn't think about whether Emily was attractive or not. She was just Emily. Even when I thought my feelings for her were changing, I don't think I thought of her as hot, or like I needed to tear her clothes off.

'Em, come here a sec,' I call. 'This is Jess. She's my... ah...'

Jess thrusts her hand out. 'I'm his roomie in London.'

My *roomie*? She's not just my roomie. I scowl at her but she ignores me, seemingly hitting it off with Emily right away. Unsurprising really since they're both pretty incredible. At least, I used to think Emily was incredible. Then I started to hate her. But now, watching her talk easily with Jess, I'm finding it hard not to remember how great she is. Twenty odd years of her being like my right arm might have something to do with that.

We eat around the outdoor table. Conversation flows. Wine flows. Whether it's relief or wine, or that Jess and Emily are getting along, I feel content. Confused, absolutely. But not weird. Which is weird.

After dinner, Brooks, Kit and I clear the table and load the dishwasher. It's the least we can do, given we've contributed in no other way. We decide during that time that we should make a fire on the beach.

Like the cavemen hunter gatherers that we so obviously are, in our tailored shorts and shirts, the three of us find wood and other scraps to use for kindling. But unlike cavemen, we light the fire with half a box of matches and a bottle of lighter fuel.

We bring a few fold-out chairs, a cool box of booze and a couple of rugs down onto the sand, then beckon the others. Becky brings down amazing cakes that ought to win awards for how stunning they look, and we pass them around with forks.

I sit on a rug with Jess by my side, sharing a cake Becky calls Opera with a Twist. Emily takes one of the fold-out chairs opposite us in the circle we have formed around the small flames. Izzy brings down her acoustic guitar.

'I am so full,' Jess moans, as she lifts another forkful of cake toward her mouth. 'But this is too good to leave.'

I dart forward, wrapping my mouth around the forkful of decadence, toppling both of us in the process so we're laughing in a boozy heap on the rug. 'Thinking of your hips, babe,' I tell her, receiving a well-earned elbow to the ribs in return.

As we sit, I catch Emily looking our way. She offers a slight and clearly forced smile, which kills the mood – at least for me. What was that about?

As Izzy starts to play her own songs, her voice soft, her words beautiful, I keep looking at Emily. Watching the way the light of the fire flickers across her skin, the way her eyes close and she rocks gently as she listens to Izzy play. I'm transported to Staten Island, sitting in our treehouse, watching her move this exact way as I played the guitar for her as a twelve-year-old kid. God, that was an easy time.

'Does anyone else want to play?' Izzy asks once she's finished another song.

'Would you mind?' Emily asks. 'I'm precious about people touching my guitar so I'd understand.'

'No, please, go ahead.'

Emily takes the Fender and puts the strap over her head. She tunes the strings to her liking and I watch her settle into the guitar the way I used to tell her to do before she starts to play. I don't realize I'm smiling until Jess prods my dimple with her finger.

Emily starts to pick the beginning of a tune I recognize. It's RaeLynn's 'The Apple.' She's always loved country.

I watch her delicate fingers move across the strings, listening to every rasp and dip of her voice as she sings. I listen to her singing about biting into an apple and how that move started to make everything she knew unravel. I know she chose the song with intention.

The thing about Emily and me is that we always struggled to talk about feelings. We knew they were there, the way we knew everything about each other, but we never put them into words. Unless we put them into music.

Is it possible for your heart to ache? If it is, that's what's happening. As I realize how much I've missed her, how a part of me has been missing for three years, my heart is aching.

Emily moves on to play RaeLynn's 'Young,' and I find myself singing along with her, both of us laughing as we hit pitchy notes. God, I've missed her so much.

But when she's finished, and the moment has passed, I remember how much she hurt me.

'Where did you learn to play like that, Emily?' Izzy asks.

Emily looks at me. 'My best friend taught me.'

'Jake?' Izzy asks, pointing the question to me. 'You play?'

Emily stands, bringing the guitar to me. 'Are you kidding? Jake is amazing on the guitar.'

'It's true,' Brooks says from his spot on the floor, leaning back between Izzy's legs as she sits in the chair behind him. 'Get the kid singing Elvis. Come on, Jakey, let's have the show.'

For some reason, I look at Jess, expecting her to be there to save me. This time, she just shrugs and sips her wine.

Shaking my head, I stand and accept the guitar from Emily with a scowl. I hook it over my shoulder, tune her up, and decide on 'Suspicious Minds.' I clear my throat and try to find my inner Elvis... tricky when I'm standing on a beach in the Hamptons barefoot, rather than on a stage in Vegas in a white jumpsuit.

'All right, here goes.'

I play that famous intro and strut my best King voice.

By the time I hit the chorus, everyone is dancing and singing around the fire, proving how much booze we've consumed. At that part of the song where the volume drops then comes back full throttle, I go all out with my show, dropping one knee to the sand, King-style.

Since I have an audience and I'm pretty wasted, I give them my best rendition of 'A Little Less Conversation'. I try not to be angry about the fact Marty has wormed his way to Jess's side and takes hold of her hands as they dance.

It's a party, Jake.

Another couple of tunes and we all settle back around the fire. I explain to Becky that I started playing the guitar when I was seven because I wanted to be in Drew and Brooks' band when I got to high school.

'Of course, that's when I was a foolish kid and I thought they were cool.'

'*Thought* we were cool?' Brooks asks. 'We *were* cool, man.'

'We had groupies,' Drew adds, as if it makes their point.

'Groupies? Brittainy Torello and Amber Hasham do not count. They clung to anything with a dick and a set of abs,' I argue.

'Buddy, at least we had abs. You were just a skinny seven-year-old who followed us around like a bad smell,' Brooks states, finishing his point with a swig of beer for emphasis.

'You were a skinny kid?' Jess asks, now sitting on a rug opposite me... and next to Marty. 'I can't imagine you skinny... not with the... you know...' I smirk as she waves a hand in the general direction of what are now very prominent abs and biceps.

'Are you blushing, Jessica Walters?' I tease.

She scowls in return.

'Ah, well, the body is thanks to Emily,' Drew says. 'See, Emily was responsible for my baby brother's first busted nose.'

Emily gasps. 'God, I remember that. Tommy Arnold.' For some reason, she looks at Jess as she tells the story. 'Tommy Arnold was a monster. He was a huge kid. He had a supernatural growth spurt or something.'

'He was also a dick,' I add.

She leans toward me, clinking her beer bottle against mine. 'Agreed. Anyway, we were walking home from school one day... Our parents always made Jake walk me home from school. We were running for some reason...'

'I said I'd race you home,' I say.

'That's right. So, we were running and Tommy Arnold stepped right out in front of me. I ran into him, then he pushed me over. And Jake saw red.' She stops directing her words at Jess and looks at me. 'You always had my back, didn't you?'

Yeah, and it turns out you didn't have mine.

'Tommy really wanted to pick a fight with me,' I say. 'He just used Emily to do it.'

'Because he knew it would get to you,' Jess says.

I shrug. 'I guess. So, Tommy and I got in a fight. He never came near Emily again and he lost his crowd of followers at school. When I got home, Brooks was there with Drew.'

Brooks nods. 'I told him, chin up, getting into a fight over a chick...'

'...is a rite of passage,' I finish, laughing. 'Then he started boxing with me, and the fine specimen of a man I am now started that day.'

'Ah, Mr Modesty made it to the party,' Jess jokes.

We share a laugh then I turn to Emily. 'Yeah, you always did have a way of getting me into trouble, Ems.'

I hear an almost wistfulness in my words. I guess I am feeling nostalgic. Life was easy back then. The worst thing about my day was pretending to hate picking Emily up from school.

'Uh, I don't think that's accurate, actually,' Emily says, her volume and confidence growing with booze. 'Name one other thing I did to get you in trouble.'

From where I'm leaning back on one elbow on the rug, I point to her. 'You're shitting me.' When she still looks incredulous, I say, 'Fine, let me see. Okay, what about Mr Hetherington's dog?'

She sucks in a breath and covers her mouth with both hands as she falls back in her beach chair. 'Oh my God, I forgot about that.'

'Yeah, I haven't.'

'What happened?' Madge asks.

Shaking my head, I share the story. 'Mr Hetherington lived on the same street as us. He had a dog. What was it called again?'

'Chippy,' Emily manages through her hysterics.

'Chippy, right. Mr Hetherington was an old man. He was a widower and used to volunteer at a library, reading to kids, for something to do. I don't know if he never house-trained Chippy or something but when he went to the library each day, he would chain Chippy up in his yard.'

'But, see, Chippy had a crush on Mrs Dawson's dog,' Emily says. 'He would pull on his chain, barking and crying, trying to get to her when she was outside.'

'Emily thought Chippy was in love with Mrs Dawson's dog,' I explain.

'He *was* in love.'

I roll my eyes. 'This one Saturday, Mr Hetherington was at the library and Chippy was going crazy outside on the chain. Mrs Dawson had gone out and left her dog in the garden.'

'In hindsight, maybe Mrs Dawson's dog was in heat,' Emily says.

'So, Emily decided she wanted Chippy to find his love and let Chippy off his leash.'

'He flew over the fence and went straight to Mrs Dawson's garden,'

Emily continues the story. 'When Mr Hetherington came home, Chippy still hadn't returned. So he started walking from house to house, asking if anyone had seen him. I was playing at Jake's when he turned up. And I've never been a good liar...'

That's a matter of opinion.

'Long story short,' I say. 'I took the fall and got into a hell of a lot of shit because Jane Austen there needed to see the dogs fall in love.'

'Wait, what happened to Chippy?' Izzy asks.

'Oh, he returned that night,' Emily says.

'And Mrs Dawson's dog?'

I look at Emily and we both start to laugh, again. 'We can't say for certain because we were grounded. But shortly after that day, Mrs Dawson had herself eight puppies.'

'And the moral of the story is...' Emily looks at me and we finish simultaneously.

'Fucking dogs in heat will lead to unwanted babies.'

I fall onto my back, laughing so hard, all I can hear is the sound of my own voice in my ears; all I can feel is the aching of my ribs.

'All right, I confess, there were a few times I shit the bed and Jake had to save my bacon. In fact, Jake did once buy me a toilet roll as a gift. Do you remember? It was the day of my finals in my second year of college. Instead of wishing me good luck, like most people would do, Jake handed me a gift bag. Inside, there was a toilet roll and a note that simply said, "Don't shit the bed, Ems".'

I prop myself back up on my elbow and take a large gulp of beer.

'How could I forget? That was the last time I spoke to you before we came here.'

Emily's joviality fades in an instant. As she looks at me, the orange glow of the fire catches the tears that fill her eyes.

What did she think? That one night here would erase everything?

She stands, dumps her empty bottle in the trash bag and screws in a smile that I know is forced.

'Well, I'm exhausted. Thank you for having me, Drew, Becky. I've had a great time.' Her voice falters as she says, 'It was nice to meet you, too, Izzy, Jess.'

She doesn't hug or kiss anyone; she leaves quickly, carrying her sandals and heading down to the beach.

The only sound is the gentle rolling of waves in the distance and the cracking of wood from the fire.

Jess gets up from her rug and comes to stand in front of me. She holds out a hand and pulls me to my feet. As she does, she tells me, 'Now is as good a time as any to talk it out, Jake.'

I know she's right but it doesn't make me want to deal with it any more. I sigh and she reaches a hand to my cheek.

'Go. If not for her, go for you.'

I drop a kiss to her brow and head down to the water's edge, catching up to Emily, who is walking the water line, rather than heading home. She must hear me as I call her name but continues her strolling pace, staring out toward the half-moon, its reflection glowing on the water's surface.

We walk until the light from Drew's place and the glow of the fire are in the distance. There's no one on the beach except us. The other beach front properties are in darkness.

I'm used to being only with Emily. I've spent half my life alone with Emily. But now, in this moment, I don't know how to be around her.

Eventually, she breaks the silence. 'I'm sorry, Jake.'

'You've said that.'

She stops and turns on the spot, holding my arms so that I'm facing her. 'And now I want to talk about what happened.'

'Why, Ems? Why discuss it three years on?'

She pushes her hands into my hair and grips, like she used to when she was mad at me.

'You're a stubborn ass, do you know that? I want to talk about it, Jake, because I want you back in my life and this is the only way I can think to make that happen. I miss you. I miss you like crazy. Not speaking to you has been like someone amputating my right leg.'

'Why your right leg?'

She laughs and I'm grateful to take the somber look from her face and the tears from her eyes.

'Any limb,' she says. 'Take your pick.'

She draws in a slow, heavy breath that makes her chest visibly rise.

'I slept with your best friend. I know we hurt you and I'm sorry. But there's nothing I can do about it.'

I take a step back from her. 'Ems, *you* were my best friend. My two closest friends were screwing each other behind my back and lying to my damn face about it. I knew things were changing between us. I thought that meant one thing and I realize now things were becoming awkward because you were lying to me. Twenty-two years, Emily. I'd known you for almost twenty-two years. I'd picked you up when you'd fallen. I'd dried your eyes when you cried. I would have done anything for you. I fucking adored you. And the whole time... the whole damn time, you were lying to me!'

She swipes her hand across her cheek and I have to fight the urge to pull her into my chest. I never have been able to stand seeing her tears. 'I know, Jake. But I, we, didn't lie to hurt you. We lied to keep from hurting you.'

My anger builds until I'm dragging a hand through my hair and pulling so hard, it hurts.

'Do you have any idea how much it killed me to walk into your room and see you two in bed together? In the apartment we shared? In the bed I'd slept in with you?'

'It's not like I hadn't walked in on you screwing people, Jake. I mean, Jesus, do you think that wasn't hard for me? There was always some girl. Someone else. Like I wasn't good enough for you.'

'That's not fair. That's when we were just friends. From the moment I thought there was something more between us, there were no other girls. Brandon *knew*. He knew how I felt. He knew that when I walked into your bedroom that night, I was going to ask you to be with me. To be mine. And the whole time, while he listened to me tell him how I felt, while we hung out together and while I thought we shared everything, you two were at it.'

She steps toward me. Close enough I can smell her scent. So close, her hair blows against my face.

'You were going to ask me to be yours?'

'Yes, Emily. I wanted to always be with you.'

She closes her eyes and presses her palms to my chest. I watch her lips as they part and I have the urge to kiss her. I don't have to fight my own want because her eyes spring open and she presses her mouth to mine. She looks into my eyes as I bring my hands to her face and slowly, tentatively, move my lips over hers.

She steps back abruptly, breaking our contact and covering her lips with her fingertips. 'I'm sorry, I shouldn't have done that.'

I don't have time to respond because she turns and runs back to her house. I don't follow her. I face out to the moon, my hands in the pockets of my jeans, my mind racing with too many thoughts to process.

Why did she kiss me? Did I kiss her back? Would I have kissed her if she hadn't got there first? Does she want me like that? Do I want her like that? Is she still the Emily I thought I knew? Am I the same Jake?

The only two things I do know are: one, I loved seeing her tonight, like old times; and two, I feel guilty as hell that that kiss just happened when Jess was yards away.

What I don't know is why I feel so damn guilty...

I turn to face the two houses. I could go to Emily. Talk it out. Work out what the hell that kiss meant to her.

Or, I could go back to Jess.

10

JAKE

God, she looks beautiful when she sleeps.

I took my time walking back along the beach, feeling every grain of sand falling between my toes, trying to decide which direction to turn.

Sitting on the edge of the bed, staring at Jess's soft cheeks, her closed eyelids, the way she looks so small curled beneath the sheets, I think I made the right decision. Tonight has shown me that Emily isn't entirely boxed away as part of my past. If I'm honest with myself, I've never wanted her to be. I felt like I had no choice but to cut her out of my life. But whatever comes of tonight, whatever happens between us, Jess is definitely my present and my future. She knows the Jake I am now better than anyone else. I know her. And I love that I do.

All of this brings back the guilt I felt on the beach.

I shouldn't feel guilty. Jess and I aren't together in that way. She's too afraid to go there. And damn it, so am I. Regardless, my stomach is wound as tight as a knot.

I go to the bathroom and shower. I rub my hands over my face under the hot water, my fingers lingering on my lips. Last time Emily kissed me like that, I was making love to her. It was seven years ago.

I open my eyes, shut off the shower, and wrap a towel around my waist.

I'm overthinking this. I'm overthinking it because I'm drunk. It was an emotionally charged situation. Nothing more.

I clean my teeth and head back into the bedroom. I pause one more time, taking in Jess, the way her hair fans across her pillow. The way the moonlight shines through the open window and highlights the natural tones of brown, the skin of her neck. And, because I'm drunk, I have the urge to kiss her right there, to nibble her skin and whisper into her ear how much I want her.

This isn't the part of the story where I confess to being into necrophilia. I'm not. At all. But I do feel like holding Jess will somehow make sense of things for me. Or at least put off the confusion until tomorrow.

I lift the sheet and slide out the spare blanket she's put down the middle of the mattress. She's persistent, I have to give her that. But I'm more persistent.

I lie back on top of the sheets in my towel and prop myself up on one elbow. I don't mean to disturb her and I have to fight the desire to trail my fingers down her bare arm.

'Are you watching me sleep?' Her eyes are still closed as she speaks.

I chuckle. 'Yes.'

'Weirdo.' She rolls over so she's facing me, matching my pose. 'You have to stop removing the blanket from the bed.'

A smirk tugs at my lips. 'I just figured, since we've both been drinking...'

'I'm going to take a wild guess that your mind is racing right now.'

'A little.' Do I tell her about the kiss? 'She apologized.'

Jess nods but stays silent. Eventually, she speaks, calmly, with reason. 'I watched the two of you together. It was nice, seeing you laugh and be happy with her. You're yourself around her.'

'I'm myself around you too.'

She smiles softly, and reaches for my hair, stroking it back from my temple. 'I know you are. That's why I also know you and Emily would hate to lose each other. She's important to you and you have a bond, Jake. Connecting with someone like that is special.'

I take her hand in mine and bring it to my lips. 'But now I have you.'

'The two don't have to be mutually exclusive. I will be your friend no matter what happens between you and Emily. I will always, always be here for you.'

It warms me to the core that she means that. I know she means it because I can't imagine ever not having her in my life either. But that *friend* word hits me somewhere new, or in a new way. And what is confusing as heck is that she and Emily would both fit that term. Yet I can't decide which one of them fits it best.

'That's a lucky thing, babe, because you're never getting rid of me.'

'Even if I shagged one of your best friends?' She laughs and for some unfathomable reason, I see the humor in her words too.

'That's close to the bone.'

'I'm sorry.'

'No, you're not. You think you're hilarious.'

'Not true. I *know* I'm hilarious.'

I shake my head. Then I bring her hand to my mouth again and tell her, 'Thank you.'

'For what?'

'For being able to see that I needed to speak to Emily. For pushing me to do it. We can't get those years back, and I'm not sure where we go from here, but you were right about us needing to talk. I realize now that I've missed her, you know.'

'Well, you're welcome. Although, I'm sure you would have gotten there on your own eventually.'

'Nice to do it before I'm gray though, huh?'

She nods.

'Now, about this screwing my friends thing... what was going on with you and Marty tonight?'

'Marty? I spoke to Marty as much as everyone else. Aww, are you worried I'm going to get myself a new friend and replace you, Jakey?'

There it is again, that alien feeling in my gut. I don't like it.

'Just watch your back, all right?'

'I don't need to watch my back, Jake. I know you have it.' She leans forward, bites the tip of my nose, then rolls back over. 'Since I'm boozed, you might as well give me a cuddle.'

I slip the towel from around my waist and slide under the sheet, tugging her back into me.

'Seriously, Jake, it's one thing having you spoon me with my knickers on but if that tail gets lost in the night...'

I bury my laughter in her neck. Then I breathe in her natural scent and close my eyes, forgetting everything else.

Her breathing starts to calm, taking mine with it. I wonder whether she's already asleep until she says, 'Elvis, huh?'

'The King,' I tell her, absentmindedly dropping my lips to her shoulder. Her next breath leaves her like a soft sigh. Then the sound of waves is all I can hear.

* * *

'Losers buy the first round of drinks tonight. And mine will be expensive,' Sarah says, from where she's standing in the middle of the circle the rest of us have formed around her on the beach.

By the time Jess and I got up this morning, it had been decided that we were playing beach games today. She and Brooks had measured sixty yards and marked start and finish lines in the sand. Personally, I'd have been happy staring at Jess half naked by the pool again but I guess the wheelbarrow race works too.

'What are the teams?' Drew asks.

'You choose a partner. Teams of two, obviously,' Sarah says.

'How about it, Jess?'

I snap my head to glare at the smug bastard that is Marty.

Jess glances to me and shrugs. 'Erm, yeah, su—'

'Jess already has a team,' I all but growl. Yeah, my inner caveman has showed up. We might just be friends, but she's not teaming up with a guy like Marty. He's bedded half the women in New York. And there's no chance I'm letting him get his filthy popsicle anywhere near the place mine calls home.

As the others pair off in twos, Sarah clips Marty around the ear. 'You're with me. And I swear to God, if you perv on my legs, I will cut off your balls and fry them like bacon.'

Jess laughs and heads to the start line with Sarah. I put a firm hand on Marty's shoulder, holding him back. Leaning into his ear, I tell him, 'Rein it in, Marty, or you and I are gonna have a big problem.'

'Shame. I was looking forward to holding her legs and riding the barrow.'

It takes every ounce of willpower I have not to punch the jackass right up in his barrow.

We take our positions at the start line and Jess bends to all fours. Hell, there was no way I was letting Marty have this view. Her cut-off Daisys barely cover the bottom of her ass cheeks. Jess lifts a leg up to me and I take hold of it, sliding my hand along her bare skin.

'Damn it, Jess, I think I need you to get drunk tonight.'

She glances over her shoulder, then winks and I swear my todger winks right back at her.

From her upside-down position, Sarah calls, 'Three. Two. One. Go.'

We set off, Jess wobbling on her arms as I drive her forward from behind. I glance left and see Edmond and Aimee, Sarah and Marty, and Drew and Becky are all in various stages of collapse and irrecoverable fits of laughter. But Brooks and Izzy are going strong. Damn those two and their bloody fitness regimes.

'Come on, Jess. We aren't letting them beat us. We're the best goddamn team I know.'

As if my angry pep talk worked, she's suddenly straighter and stronger and we're charging to the finish line. Then Izzy topples and I'm so busy gloating that I let Jess topple too.

'Piggybacking it!' Brooks calls.

I haul Jess from the sand, throwing her onto my back. Then it's Brooks and me racing with the girls on our backs. Jess is squealing as I sprint as fast as I can. I've got one eye on the line, the other on Brooks.

'We're neck and neck,' Jess shouts.

With the line in reach, I launch myself at it as if I'm going for a touchdown. I throw one hand out full stretch and put the other behind me to stop Jess from hitting her head against me. When we're down, Jess rolls off me. Both of us lie on our backs, laughing so much, it hurts.

'Are you okay?' I ask.

Through her breathlessness, she manages to say she's fine. I roll over to her with the intention of helping her up. But she takes me by surprise, her laughter fading into something entirely different. Something intense. Something I only see in her when she's drunk. And I'm blinded by it.

I brush the hair from her face and drop my gaze to her red lips. Then I remember Emily's lips on mine last night. I close my eyes and swallow down everything that's balled in my throat.

I stand and help Jess to her feet.

'Did we win?' Jess calls to Sarah, her voice faltering slightly. She doesn't look at me as she heads over to the group.

Why do I get the feeling I'm fucking up on all fronts?

And why in hell do I keep wanting to be close to Jess, needing to touch her, kiss her, like I need air and water, like my life depends on her?

I pick up my cap from the sand and head over to Sarah for our next instruction. Jess bumps her hip against mine and gives me a small smile. 'We won.'

It might be a small victory but I'll take it.

I wrap my arm around her shoulders. 'Of course we did, babe. We're like Maverick and Goose.'

'Bonnie and Clyde,' she says.

'Sonny and Cher.'

Nah, we're good. This stuff with Emily has just got me freaking out.

*　*　*

We're sitting on white chairs on the patio of a bar not far from Drew's pad. The wind is kicking up from the beach and blowing white chiffon sheets that hang from the terrace frame. The sun is setting before us, burning orange, turning the farthest clouds shades of pink as it descends.

A live singer and guitarist are playing soft rock inside. The sound is a perfect backdrop to the evening.

Brooks has bought the first round of Tequila Sunrises: Jess's suggestion. That woman loves her tequila. But considering we played men versus women at softball and we let the girls win, basically all of the rounds are on the guys tonight.

The evening is easy. Brooks brings me up to speed on the opening of his second Brooks Adams gym in the city. Izzy talks about her latest audition for a musical and how she has a paid gig coming up in a café-cum-bar in Hell's Kitchen in a few weeks, her first paid gig since she moved to New York. And Drew and Marty tell us about their plans for the firm. Mostly, they bitch at each other about the things one does that the other doesn't and vice versa. I point out the obvious: that it's a good thing they're two halves of a team.

It really is nice here. Growing up, I think we once made it to the Hamptons for a day trip. I vaguely remember the beach and sitting in Pop's truck for what seemed like forever, squished between Drew and our sister, Millie. In part, we probably didn't visit because we lived right on Staten Island's South Beach. More than that, we didn't have the money to come on weekend breaks to places like the Hamptons.

I know that people say money can't buy happiness and all that. But have you ever noticed that the people who say that stuff are billionaire philanthropists and such like? I definitely do think being happy is more important than being wealthy, as odd as it might sound since I work in investments, thereby making rich people richer, but I also don't walk around with my eyes closed. You have to have a certain amount of money. It's like Maslow's hierarchy of needs. Business and economics school 101. You need food, sex, air and water. Then you need to build on that. Have a steady income, self-esteem. When you have all the lines in Maslow's triangle checked off, you can officially be happy. And guess what: you need money to buy food.

I'm proud to look around the table and see my brother and Brooks. Me. Jess. We didn't come from anything and now, we're sitting here drinking tequila cocktails in one of the finest parts of the world.

Yeah, I'm pretty damn content. I'm not thinking about what Emily and I were, what we ought to be or whether that kiss meant anything. Yes, I want to understand what's different between my friendship with Emily and the one I have with Jess, but I don't need to know tonight. I'm just... peaceful.

'What are you smiling at, sweet cheeks?' Jess leans in, nudging me in the side on our two-seat sofa.

I lift my arm, encouraging her under it. 'What's not to smile about?' I press my lips to her head and she falls deeper into my side.

'Amelie, how do you like your new place?' I ask, remembering that she and Edmond moved to the suburbs not long ago.

'I adore it,' she says, resting her cocktail on the low table in the middle of our group. 'It needed some work but we are almost finished with the reconstruction. Edmond had the kitchen designed to look...'

I lose her next words when I see Emily walk into the bar. She has on capris pants and a loose, lemon-colored blouse. Her hair is drawn back into a braid. I wait for some kind of feelings to come. Something to help me make sense of what happened on the beach last night. But I feel nothing; I'm happy to see her and that's all. I'm about to call her over when a guy I know too well walks into the place and over to the bar where she's waiting to be served.

My legs force me to stand without waiting for my brain to tell them to stay the hell down. My old roommate and college buddy. The one who screwed Emily, knowing how I felt about her. The one who listened to me tell him how my feelings for her were changing. How I didn't want to leave college without her, without us being together. And the whole goddamn time, he was screwing her.

'That son of a bitch.'

Every muscle in my body goes rigid and I roll my jaw as my fists clench at my sides. It's about time I taught this guy a life lesson.

Brandon slides his arm up Emily's back and leans in to kiss her. Her eyes flick to me and I see the same shock on her face that I'm feeling right now.

'She's still screwing him?'

'Jake, sit down.' I hear Drew's voice but can't take my eyes off of the scene in front of me. The scene that's taking me back three years. The one that tore my fucking heart open.

'Jake, we gonna have trouble, man?' Brooks asks.

I can't respond because my legs are moving me forward. Emily says something to the bastard and he turns to see me. His eyes widen.

Yeah, buddy, you better be fucking afraid. I've waited three years for this.

From nowhere, my vision is blocked by someone stepping in front of me. That same person takes firm hold of my cheeks in her palms and crashes her mouth against mine.

I don't kiss Jess back. Too stunned and confused to think.

'Kiss me, Jake. Kiss me,' she whispers.

I look into her eyes. She's sober. I'm sober. I'm also fucking raging, and yet desperate for her to kiss me like that again. Rage, testosterone, and sheer burning desire for this woman crash together and I press my lips against hers, closing my eyes to drown in her taste. To lose myself in the touch of her tongue against mine when I part her lips. She groans into my mouth and I reply with my own.

There's no one else in the bar except us and my loud thoughts about my desire to take her home. My desperation. That's all I can hear.

I push my fingers into her long hair and find her nape, pulling her to me, needing more of her.

Whistles and the sound of cheering force us apart. We stand on the spot, facing each other, both breathing hard. Then she asks, 'Are you good?'

I have no idea what the meaning of that question is, so I can't answer.

She nods anyway and says, 'Yeah, so good. You're good. I'm good. Everybody's good.'

I'm still rooted to the spot as she pats me on the arm, like a coach telling his pitcher to have a good game, and she goes back to our table.

I glance to the bar and see Emily and Brandon have disappeared. I adjust my cap, run a hand along my stubble-covered jaw, and turn to join the others.

Clearing my suddenly dry throat, I sit on the sofa next to Jess, resting my forearms on my knees and needlessly fiddling with the peak of my cap.

Sarah finally starts up a conversation, breaking the silence around the table. I turn my head to look at Jess and ask, for her ears only, 'What was that?'

'I was saving you from yourself. Thank me or forget about it,' she snaps, in a way that's not like her.

I narrow my eyes, trying to read her tone, her body language, her mind. I can't make sense of anything any more.

She turns on a smile and briefly takes part in the conversation.

I sit back in my seat and watch her. That kiss was... What was that kiss?

After a few minutes, Jess flutters her hand in front of her cheek. 'Gosh, I'm a little warm. I'm going to see if I can catch some breeze for a few minutes.'

It's as if she is saying the words to herself because she looks at no one, just gets up, grabs her cocktail and walks toward the end of the deck, even though there's plenty of breeze where we are. She rests her forearms on the fencing and looks out to sea. Her shoulders seem to deflate. I'm about to stand and go to her when Sarah beats me to it.

'I think I'll join her,' she says, giving me a look that makes me feel like I'm not invited. She drops a hand to Drew's shoulder in a way that says, *I've got this*.

I'm glad someone understands what the hell is going on.

'Help me get more drinks?' Drew asks. I know he wants to talk. Usually, it wouldn't be my thing but right now, if someone wants to even point me in the right direction, I'll follow willingly.

Drew puts in the order and I lean back on the bar, looking out to where Jess and Sarah stand, shoulder to shoulder in the gray light of dusk.

While the server mixes up twelve margaritas, Drew rests an arm on the bar, facing me. 'Should we start with the truth of what happened between you and Emily or what's going on with you and Jess?'

'Before this week, I thought I had one old best friend and one new best friend; does that satisfy your curiosity?'

He shrugs. 'What exactly do you have now?'

I shake my head slowly. 'If I could answer that question, I probably wouldn't have watched both women run away from me just now.'

'Was that Brandon who walked in here with Emily? Your old college roommate?'

I nod. Too furious to talk about him yet. 'Yeah, that's the dickhead I used to live with.'

'He's with Emily?'

'What did it look like?' I snap.

He holds up a hand. 'All right. Let's park that one for now until you calm down. Why don't we talk about what's got you in a mess with the Brit?'

I take off my cap and replace it, grumbling in the process. 'Nothing, I guess. We're friends. She was trying to stop me from being a jackass in the middle of a bar and, I don't know, maybe in front of Emily.'

'Jesus, I thought I got women mixed up sometimes. That kiss might have started out as a way to stop you from brawling in a bar but it wasn't all she was doing. That was a possessive kiss if ever I saw one. Jess was marking her territory. You're blind if you can't see what this is about for her.'

'You've got her wrong, Drew. She's here because I asked her to come. I knew seeing Emily would dredge up a truckload of stuff I haven't dealt with and probably should have in the last three years. I trust Jess implicitly. I wanted her to stop me from doing something stupid. That's what she was doing. She was being a good friend.'

Drew shakes his head but lets it lie and carries four of our drinks back toward the table. I stay put, watching as Sarah leans her temple against Jess's. She's upset. And I'm no idiot. There was more to that kiss than being a good friend. There had to have been more because I felt it. I felt it like a wave crashing over me. Hitting me with such ferocity, it turned me inside out.

Jess has more walls around her than a fort. And I... I don't know what I want. I only know I can't lose her.

So, maybe, we do what she says. I act grateful that she intervened before my fist met Brandon's jaw in a public place, and I forget everything I just felt in that kiss. I don't dwell on the fact I felt more in those thirty seconds than I felt when Emily kissed me on the beach, or even when I made love to her all those years ago.

It was only a kiss. We're friends.

And I will not lose my best friend again.

11

JAKE

We walk back along the beach. Once our eyes adjust to the darkness after the lights of the bar, the moon is enough to show us the way home. I can tell you something for nothing: it's not only the soft sand that's making our footsteps a little wobbly. No, some of the miscoordination definitely has to do with the lethal combination of Tequila Sunrise, margaritas, mojitos, daiquiris and... God knows what else, I can't think beyond that.

Whatever we had, we're all happily drunk. Jess eventually chilled out and we brushed over that kiss. Now, she's walking under my arm as we slur and laugh our way back. But I can comprehend enough to know I'm holding her up, not the other way around, and that kiss is still lingering on my lips, like a fire that smolders long after the flames have gone out. And the alcohol fog is doing nothing to stop my thoughts roaming. In fact, it's making my need to take Jess all night long worse than ever.

Unfortunately for me, I'm certain the brunette beauty under my arm is going to pass out as soon as I help her out of her denim shorts and into those sexy silks.

Unless... maybe she doesn't pass out. Maybe I get her home quickly and...

I drop my arm to her stomach and lift her over my shoulder. She squeals as I run from the others. When I think they're out of ear shot, I spank her ass so hard, she screams again.

'I've waited days for this fine ass, Jess. I'm taking you to my bed and I'm going to make you—'

Running onto the decking in front of the pool, I almost crash into Emily. She sits on the steps coming down from the pool side, still in her clothes from the bar, her arms wrapped around her knees.

I bring Jess down to the decking, my thoughts suddenly jumping from taking Jess to bed to wondering what on earth Emily is doing here.

'I, erm, I'm drunk. I'm just going to...' Jess waves a hand in the general direction of the house and offers Emily a soft smile as she slides past her and heads up the stairs. She glances back to me and I feel like I'm at another crossroads. I want nothing more than to follow Jess to bed. To go at her all night, then hold her in my arms until the sun comes up.

But here's Emily. My past. My lifelong best friend.

'Can we talk?' she asks, stealing my attention.

Jess steps toward the house. I watch her go.

'You know, Emily, I don't think we can. There's a great girl up there, who I fucking love being around. Who's never lied to me and who doesn't deserve to be caught up in our shit. And, frankly, I'm over it. I'm over our past and our whole damn story.'

'Jake, please.' She steps toward me, placing her hand over my fore-arm. 'Two minutes.'

'Why, Ems? So you can lie to me some more?'

'No, I just...' She pauses as the others come around the bushes and into view. Their boisterous conversation stops. This is their vacation too and I'm not about to ruin it.

'Fine. Two minutes.' I nod to the beach and Emily follows me.

We stand at the water's edge, water lapping our feet, the way it was when she kissed me last night.

'Go ahead. Talk. Tell me why you didn't tell me that you're still seeing that dick.'

'Quit it, Jake. You're better than this.'

'Am I? I don't feel better. When he walked into that bar with you tonight, I wanted to rip to his head off.'

'Jake, we can't help that we fell for each other!'

'Fell for each other? You kissed me last night!'

'Yeah, I did, Jake. But you kissed me back. And tonight, you're kissing Jess!'

'Leave Jess the hell out of this.'

'Why? Because you've fallen for your best friend, again?'

'What Jess and I have is not what you and I had.'

She softens her tone. 'But you have fallen for her. You've fallen for someone you weren't supposed to. See, it happens, Jake. We fall in love when we least expect it and sometimes with the people we don't mean to.'

'I'm not talking about Jess and me. I'm talking about you and Brandon, going behind my back. And don't blame love or the damn Cupid effect, Ems. You were the two people I trusted most. My closest friends. You went behind my back and you...'

Ripped my heart out.

'Don't blame love for what happened last night. You kissed me. What kind of love is that?'

She nods and settles her gaze on her bare toes in the sand. 'I know. I did kiss you.' She takes a deep breath and turns to look out to sea. 'I do love him. But I love you too. I always have. I think it's possible that he's the man I'm supposed to be with but that you're my soulmate, Jake. I want to love him with all of me, I do. But then I saw you here and I thought maybe it was a sign. Like I'd found you again and—'

'Stop it, Emily. I won't let you put me in a spin again.'

'I'm not trying to do that. I... I just don't think I can live without you, Jake. I need you in my life. I don't think I can love Brandon unless we're okay. And... if... if I can only have you by us being together or me not being with him...'

I pull off my cap and drag a hand through my hair, exhaling loud enough to be heard above the sound of the waves.

'I want you in my life too,' I admit to her, and myself. I turn to stand by her side, both of us looking out to the same dark horizon. 'But not like that. I don't want to give you an ultimatum.'

Would she really give him up, the man she says she loves, for me?

The thought weighs heavily on my shoulders and I'm suddenly exhausted. By us. Our whole story.

'Go home, Emily.'

I don't look back as I walk to the house. The lights are out inside but I hear voices as I come up the path to the patio. Under the light of outdoor lanterns, I see Drew and Brooks sitting in two garden chairs. Brooks' guitar rests against his seat.

Then it hits me: the distinct, sweet smell of weed. I sniff as I get closer. I see the joint Brooks passes to my brother as he leans his head back and exhales white smoke. Ah, how I'd enjoy the heady fog of marijuana right now.

'You boys smoking without me?'

'Here he is. Casanova,' Brooks says, chuckling in a way that's not much like him. A way that tells me he's already getting high.

I hook my finger, beckoning Drew to hand over the joint. I take it from him and sit on the deck, one knee pulled up to my chest. It's been a while since I smoked weed. None of us have ever been big on it but... I take my first drag, taking it back, feeling it fill my lungs and disperse into my body.

I hand the joint to Brooks and finally get my thoughts out loud. 'You two sitting up, putting the world to rights, while everyone else is in bed. Smoking weed. Something you only do when you have something to celebrate. So, boys, what are we celebrating?'

Brooks pulls on the joint, turning the end orange. 'Not my call, man,' he says.

I look to my brother. His lip curls at one side, giving me that smile I learned from him. Cool as ice.

'I'll tell you, kid. But first, it's about time you leveled about what went down with you and Emily.'

I reach out and take the smoke from Brooks, cocking my head to one side as I take another hit, knowing full well that the glint in my eye is a match for my brother's.

Exhaling a plume of smoke, feeling my head get a little lighter, I tell him, 'All right, I'll tell you about Emily. And once I'm through, you can admit that we're sitting out here getting stoned because you're going to propose to Becky.'

I lean over and hand Drew the joint. He meets my eye, then takes it from me with that slick smirk. 'You always were too smart for your own good.'

'Yeah, well, that's thanks to you, huh?'

His eyes narrow as he sobers and stares at me.

'Come on, I know you paid for me to go to college. I'm not stupid. I just want you to say it so I can thank my brother for the best thing anyone has ever done for me.'

He swallows hard, his Adam's apple pulling the skin of his neck taut.

'Mom doesn't ever need to know you know, Jake.'

I nod. 'I'm with you.' I stand and move in front of my brother, holding out my hand. He stands, taking hold of my forearm with his free hand. I pull him into me and wrap my arm around him. 'I fucking love you, Drew.'

'I'd do anything for you, Jake. You know that.'

'Yeah, I do. And the same goes for you.' I pull back from him and slap a hand against his cheek, letting it linger. 'As for you for marrying Becky, I couldn't be happier for you, seriously. She's great.'

He wraps his hand around the nape of my neck and shakes me once, hard. He points at me, the joint between his fingers. 'Not a word.'

'My lips are sealed.'

Drew passes the joint to Brooks and sits back in his wicker chair. I sit down on the deck, then pull my knees up and put my hands behind my head as I lie back, staring up at the star-studded sky.

'So, when's the big moment?'

'I don't know yet. But Millie and Mom would kill me if I didn't let them celebrate with us, and they're coming here on Saturday night, which means...'

'You better get a move on,' Brooks finishes, handing the weed down to me.

As we pass the joint and Brooks lights another, I can feel myself slipping into peace. I feel my body sinking into the deck. The sky and the stars seem to move closer.

'Emily shagged Brandon.' The words leave me on a sigh.

'Yeah, I figured as much when they walked into the bar together tonight,' Drew says. 'Who are you pissed at, him or her?'

'Both. Him for knowing how I felt about her and doing it anyway. Her for... hell, I don't even know.' I close my eyes and feel myself drift more as the weed keeps moving through my system. 'They were at it for months and neither one of them told me. Regardless of anything I felt about her, or that I thought she felt about me, it's the lies that I can't stand. She was my best friend and I thought Brandon was a good guy.' I open my eyes to take the joint from Brooks. 'I think I'm pissed at myself too, for not seeing it. For not... for not doing anything about Emily sooner.'

'Ever wondered why you didn't?' Brooks asks.

I turn my head to the side and look at him. 'What do you mean?'

'You loved Emily; everyone knew that. But you never went for anything more. Maybe work out why you didn't. You need to figure out why you decided something had changed. Maybe once you've done that, you'll be able to put this mess to bed and get your friend back.'

'Brooks, I swear to God, you're the Dalai Lama,' Drew says, and we all laugh.

'When did you turn into a shrink?' I ask.

'I'm no shrink, man. I just had to pull my head out of my ass younger than most people. Now I have a teenage daughter to contend with and need to be both Dad and counselor.'

'Yeah, that's what you get when you knock your girlfriend up at sixteen,' I say.

Silence falls between us for seconds before Brooks laughs, hard, throwing his head back. Then Drew and I are laughing with him. We laugh for so long, I can't even remember what was funny.

When we calm, Brooks picks up his guitar. I close my eyes as he starts to strum, then he sings a Brantley Gilbert track. The natural huskiness he's always had in his voice, even when he and Drew had their high-school band and Brooks sang lead, is still there. But with age, his voice has deepened, and whether it's the weed, the stars, the light breeze coming off the ocean, or being in the company of two men I love and respect, I drift as he sings, until my entire body is weightless.

When the song comes to an end, Brooks strums slowly and softly, to no particular tune.

'God, I've missed New York and being close to you guys,' I confess, as much to myself as them.

'You can always come home, Jake,' Drew says.

I could. But home is also England, with Jess. 'I couldn't leave her.'

Neither one of them responds and as Brooks starts singing again, I'm left to think about how much I mean those words. I couldn't leave her. I'd never want to. She's only yards away from me and I miss her. Is that possible?

When Brooks kicks into the chorus of Blake Shelton's 'Mine Would Be You,' I join in without conscious thought. Drew does too. And we're all singing until I start to laugh.

'I'm finally part of the band. It only took sixteen years.'

'And you're still not cool enough,' Brooks says, breaking the song. Hell, we're at it again, laughing through the start of a third joint. 'Why is everything hilarious when you add weed to the equation?'

My question goes unanswered because Brooks suddenly switches his beat and all three of us are screaming out the word's to Wheatus's 'Teenage Dirtbag.' We sound like cats in heat but, damn, we're having a good time.

'This is possibly the worst thing we've ever heard!'

I open my eyes and look at the upstairs window of the house to find the source of those words. Sarah, Izzy, Becky and Jess are leaning out of one of the bedroom windows.

'Get your ass down here,' Brooks shouts.

We next see them as they come onto the deck, all in some variation of lounge wear. Jess is still in her tiny denim shorts but now she has one of my hoodies on, drowning her slim frame.

'Can I smell weed?' Sarah asks, standing in bed shorts and furry booties, her hands on her hips.

'It's even harder than usual to take you seriously,' I tell her from the ground beneath her.

'Shut up, you. And you!' She points to Drew. 'Pass that thing over here.' Sarah pulls on the joint and starts passing it around.

Becky and Izzy refuse but Jess holds out her hand. 'Hell yes. I haven't smoked weed since... ha, since I got ditched at the altar.'

She sits on the decking next to me, her legs crossed beneath her. Her bare thigh is too much temptation. As I take her in, her long, soft hair, my clothes on her, I rest a hand on her thigh.

Jess exhales. I don't know what it is about her leaning back, the skin of her neck stretched taut as she blows out smoke, that is unbelievably sexy. The ultimate temptation. Jesus, as if I wasn't horny enough earlier.

'No way,' Sarah says. 'You were ditched at the altar?'

Jess nods. 'Yep. I was already in the dress, my hair was done. My aunt and I were waiting for my uncle to come get me. My uncle knocked on my bedroom door but as soon as I opened it, I knew something wasn't right. He looked at me like...'

She shakes her head and I tighten my grip on her thigh. She never talks about this. I know she'll be reliving it and hurting. I know she's never gotten over it. This, her parents, it's all part of the cage she's built around her heart.

'He had this look, like he thought he was about to break my heart. He stepped into the room and instead of linking my arm through his and leading me toward my husband-to-be, he pulled me into his chest and said, "Jess, my gorgeous girl, one day there's going to be a man who deserves all of you." And I never saw my fiancé again.'

Everything stops. Brooks even stops playing. Then Sarah stands up and hands Jess the joint again. 'Here, you need this more than I do.'

Jess laughs.

'It was my fault really. I knew I wasn't... that I could never... ah, never mind.'

'Good fucking riddance,' Sarah adds, making Jess's body shudder with humor again.

'Thanks, Sarah.'

'So, he drove you to weed, huh?'

'Possibly,' Jess says, studying the joint. 'It might have been my aunt who gave me the idea. She smoked medicinally.'

'Oh, gosh, Jess, that's awful,' Sarah says. 'What was wrong with her?'

'She was addicted to weed.'

Even though I know Jess well enough to appreciate she was covering her hurt with humor, she has us all guffawing. Brooks starts playing again, something cheerier this time. I sit up enough to pull Jess down to the ground, so she's lying on my chest. I press my lips to her head.

'He must have been fucking crazy,' I tell her. 'If I ever got you in a white dress, I'd be there at the altar and every other day for the rest of my life.'

I'm trying to comfort her; she'll know it. But as I lie here, stroking her hair, feeling her press against me, I mean every single word. Any man would be lucky to have Jess. She's been through so much, and I don't know a stronger, more independent woman, even if she has had to build walls to protect herself. I swallow the lump that forms in my throat at the thought of any other man managing to break down those walls. Do the thing I haven't been able to do.

Before I can consider how hard I've really tried, Izzy and Becky start to shout about The Beatles and Brooks starts to play 'Let it Be.'

I pin Jess to my chest as we all get stoned and sing into the darkness of the early morning.

12

JESS

It's probably clear by now that I believe in signs. No, not signs, but *something*. Some kind of power. That belief has certainly been heightened by my aunt and uncle, and the time they've made me spend trying to 'find myself.' But it started before then. It started with my parents and my understanding of why one of them couldn't exist without the other. But how's this for an invisible form, or a sign, if you prefer...

It had been years since I had met Danny Dukkha – that's what I decided to call him after our first meeting the morning of the alms-giving ceremony in Laos. I was nineteen and celebrating my birthday at a beach shack bar in Bali. I wasn't alone because I was in a bar full of backpackers who were willing to take tequila shots with me. But in terms of having anyone close to me, anyone who actually knew it was my birthday and that was why I was feeling the light buzz of my first four shots, I was on my own.

I was sitting on a wood swing, in place of a bar stool, turning my empty glass in my fingers on the bar top. Ruth and John were on a trek in the mountains somewhere, and I'm fairly certain they had forgotten it was my birthday in any event. The sun had long since gone down and fire candles lit the beach out front of the bar, but I was still wearing the kaftan I'd made myself and had been wearing all afternoon. I was still wearing the cowboy hat some guy I briefly flirted with a few weeks back gave me when he left for his next destination – Australia, I think he was headed to.

I must have looked quite sad. I was. I remember I was contemplating whether I should be celebrating that I had managed to live another year, or whether I should be mourning the fact I was one year closer to the young age my parents were when they died. That's when it happened.

'*Dukkha.*' A voice came from over my shoulder, close to my ear, making me jump. Yet I didn't turn because I thought I recognized that voice. And it made me freeze.

For years, I had contemplated the words Danny Dukkha had said to me in Laos. I had come to understand what he meant by being in a constant state of suffering in the cycle of the Buddhist interpretation of karma. He didn't know me, yet that day, he knew I was clinging to something I could never hold on to, and he was telling me that it would lead to me suffering until I was reborn.

I had thought about Danny a lot since that day in Laos. So tell me it wasn't some kind of sign that he had found me in Bali, after no connection since Laos, and he was whispering into my ear as I celebrated my birthday alone.

He pulled out my swing an inch and I rocked forward. I was so busy trying to get my head around what was happening, I was surprised by the smile that took over my lips.

'You got more beautiful, if it's possible,' he said, and my lips spread wider still.

He signaled to the barman, holding up two fingers, as he straddled a wooden swing next to me, and sat down facing me.

'Danny Dukkha,' I eventually said. His name left me as part of an exhale.

'You remember.'

Remember? He'd been in my thoughts so many times. 'Yeah, I remember. What on earth are you doing here?'

'Same as you, I suspect.' He took one of the shot glasses filled with tequila that the bartender had set down. 'What are we drinking to?'

I don't know why I told him, when I hadn't mentioned it to anyone else, but I said, 'It's my birthday.'

He nodded and handed me the second glass. We took the shot, laughing as we winced through the burn of the cheap, beachside tequila. 'Happy birthday,' he said, his face contorted as he spoke, then he shook his head.

I laughed, a little deliriously, and I still don't know why his presence made me so happy that night. The coincidence? Having company when I had been feeling alone? That he stopped me from pondering life and death and made me smile? Or that I had possibly been waiting to confront him about his thoughts on karma from years before?

But that night, it didn't matter. We talked and laughed. He told me everywhere he had been in the world since we'd last met and I told him where I had been dragged. Between us, we had covered six continents, forty countries with five near-death experiences.

After a few more tequilas, Danny ordered two bottles of water and we walked on the beach. Under the firelights, we drank our water and talked more. He asked questions about me. About my thoughts and feelings. About the clothes I made. And it was a revelation. Someone wanted to know about me and seemed to care about the answers. And he was fascinating. The guy who seemed to have no troubles and wanted to travel the world, not interested in growing roots anywhere. He was my polar opposite, and it was refreshing.

Age had changed him, made him broader, taller. His arms and legs were more tanned under his short-sleeved shirt and board shorts. There was more character about his face. *Being in his twenties suits him*, I thought. He was more attractive than I remembered. But more than anything, I liked the combination of youth and worldliness about his eyes. He had bright irises that seemed incredibly alive, but he had an abundance of knowledge and wisdom for such a young guy.

'The wisdom comes from being an explorer,' he said.

I was sitting next to him in the sand, my knees pulled in to my chest, my hair blowing in the warm Balinese wind. I laughed. 'An explorer? You make yourself sound like Gulliver.'

He smiled but he said, 'That's what I am. And, you know something? I don't ever want to be anything else.'

'You don't? Truthfully? I mean, don't you ever think about what you're going to do with your life?'

He chuckled then and lay back in the sand, his hands behind his head. 'I am doing things with my life, Jess. I write travel articles and sell them. I work bar jobs here and there. People would kill to see the world the way we do.'

I stared out to sea and sighed. I knew that, of course. I knew in many ways, I was insanely lucky to see and experience the things I did.

'But don't you ever feel nomadic? You think of yourself as an explorer and I... I can't help but think of myself as homeless.'

'The world is your home, Jess.'

I stared at him then, the firelight flickering across his face, and I wished I could be like him. I wished in some ways that I had never seen the perfect home life; then I might not crave it. But I had and I did. I craved the bond my parents had shared. I wanted to feel the unconditional love of family. I craved the way my parents had loyal friends who would always help them out when they needed it and laugh and joke with them when they needed to be picked up. I longed for that kind of happiness and I feared it.

As I stared at Danny, I started to think if I could only be more like him, I might be happier.

That night, Danny and I made love quietly in his hostel bed. For four weeks, we were inseparable. We made love, we took treks in the Balinese jungle. We ate like the Balinese. We explored the islands, truly. We meditated with my aunt and uncle. The four of us did yoga at sunset. It was the first time since my mum had died that I felt like I had a someone. It was nice waking up with him in the morning, even in sleeping bags and old tents. It was nice to hold someone's hand. I enjoyed not making every decision about where to visit each day by myself.

Danny was confident and worldly. He found me a market stall where I sold my clothes, the first time I had actually made money from something I had made. He convinced me I should try to write a travel, fashion and food blog. That might not seem edgy these days but eleven years ago, it was very new age and something I never would have thought about doing if it weren't for Danny.

He was great for me. He brought me out of my *turtle shell*, as he called it. And even though I would never give up the dream of having roots one day, he made colors seem brighter, sounds sharper, and every experience somehow felt more alive. I felt like I understood the world more and life. There was a part of me that was almost happy.

'He makes you smile,' Aunt Ruth said one day when we were taking a dip in the pool of waterfalls. 'I like him.'

It was the same day that Danny told me he was moving on soon. I dove under the water to wet my hair and kicked back up to the surface.

'He's leaving,' I told her. I shouldn't have let it upset me; I knew that. People leave. Bad things happen. I knew as much. But I couldn't change the fact that I felt it in my heart. The heart I had thought solely existed to pump oxygen around my body. The heart I thought was otherwise redundant.

I saw concern in Ruth's face. A rare thing, which told me she knew how much I had enjoyed having Danny around while we were here.

'Where is he going?' she asked.

'New Zealand. He's taking a campervan from Christchurch and driving around for a few months, or until he gets bored. He has lined up some farm work for a few weeks, which should pay for the van.'

Ruth nodded, contemplatively. 'You could go.'

I felt my brows scrunch. 'Go?'

Leave the only people in the world I knew and run off with a man I'd known for four weeks and one day?

'You mean to New Zealand?'

She shrugged. 'You're nineteen. You can fend for yourself. And Danny is very well-traveled.'

'But... it would just be us. We'd be, like, together.' I could feel panic whirring in my chest. Not wanting it to show, I slipped under the water and held my breath. *Keep control, Jess. Stop panicking. You're fine.* I heard my mum's voice then. It carried through the water and hit my ears. *Just breathe, angel. Breathe.* I breeched the surface and took an enormous breath, as if I were being born from the water. My heart rate calmed and for the rest of the day, I contemplated going to New Zealand with Danny. I had never been with anyone since my parents. Sure, I was dragged from place to place by Ruth and John but I was always my own person, left to my own devices. Being with Danny would be very different.

Two days later, with a necklace made of flowers in place of a ring, Danny took to his knee in the sand and proposed.

He offered to show me more of the world. He offered to be my someone, and I knew in the way he looked at me, the way he touched me when there was no need, the way he spoke to me so warmly, that he meant every word of his proposal. He loved me. I felt his love. It made me swallow my fear and say yes to him.

The days that followed were a blur. Ruth and I spent hours making my wedding dress and the flower wreath for my hair, discussing what food to buy from the local market, and which beach to use for the ceremony.

'Are you telling your family?' I asked Danny the night before our wedding, as we lay in a wood hut that Ruth and John had paid for.

He stroked my bare arm as I rested on his chest. 'I'll tell them afterward,' he said.

He didn't offer more and I didn't ask. It made me sad that his parents and siblings lived in the world and he didn't care enough to see them or to tell them he was getting married. It concerned me that he perhaps chose not to say anything because they would try to talk him out of it – after all, it was crazy. But it never occurred to me that he didn't tell them because he didn't love me. I knew he did.

He held me tight against his chest and drifted to sleep, his breathing so quiet, all I could hear was the sound of waves on the beach on which we would be married in a matter of hours. As I lay there, my chest started to tighten and I knew, no matter how much my mum's voice came to me, this was one attack I wouldn't be able to fight.

I slipped from under Danny's arm, my entire torso and throat feeling like they were swelling, like it was impossible to expand them and take in air. But inside the swelling, my diaphragm was out of control.

The fear that gripped me in those moments of panic is indescribable. I had learned to live with the attacks but for those moments, the moments when I was back in a hospital room watching my dad's own body drown him, I was terrified.

I staggered onto the sand and looked left and right as I held my hands over my chest, willing air to come. In the moon's light, I could see I was alone, and I let myself break.

I fell to my knees and I sobbed, dragging in ragged breaths as I braced my body on all fours. And I remember thinking, *There's nothing I wouldn't give to have my parents back. To be part of their family. Part of something, something that never had to end because we were just too happy.*

See, the fundamental difference between Danny and me was that he thought I couldn't be happy because I constantly aspired to achieve something that I would never reach. In his mind, life was a circle of birth, suffering, death and rebirth. I thought differently, and I still do.

I heard him run toward me, calling my name, and I felt his arms as he slid his legs around me and held my back to his chest. There, I found my breath and I found a calmer state.

'What is it, Jess? Talk to me,' he said into my neck, as he stroked tears from my cheeks.

I explained to him then, 'My circle of life is different to yours, Danny. I don't believe in rebirth. I believe I suffer but not because I am trying to achieve something intangible, the love my parents shared. I suffer because life's circle can only contain so many elements. There's a finite amount of each. There's a finite amount of happiness and unhappiness in the circle. My parents used up their happiness and they had to suffer for it. I used up my happiness when I was a girl and now I can't have any more.'

'Jess, you're not making sense. There is no cut off of happiness. It is what you want it to be. You can break the cycle of rebirth by being happy. Don't you see that? Let yourself be happy, end the *Dukkha*, then you can live in that state.'

I took a breath. 'Oh, Danny, life doesn't work that way. You forget that everyone has to move on. You have to leave the circle of life at some point and drift into the unknown, move beyond the circle. And it isn't rebirth. You go on as you were, just in another place, a place where you're allowed to start your count of happiness again. There are flaws in your theories, Danny.'

He kissed my hair over and over. 'What are you saying, Jess? I love you.'

'I know. I know you do, Danny, and I think I love you too. But I'm trying to tell you that I will never be truly happy. I will never be able to love the way my parents did and the way you deserve to be loved. Even if I could, don't you see, something would happen. To you, or me, or both of us. Something would have to happen to balance our happiness. Whether it's your theory or mine, can't you see they both lead to the same conclusion?'

'Jess, stop it. You need to go to sleep. Tomorrow, I am marrying you. I want to spend my life with you, and I want to spend my life helping you find your happiness.'

I cried again because I knew I wouldn't be able to make him understand. He held me as I sobbed, knowing that I couldn't say no to him because I did love him and he deserved to be happy, even if it was with me. But also hating myself for not being able to walk away, because if we got married, he would never be loved the way he loved me. Because if I allowed myself to fall, something would happen. We would get sick. I couldn't stand the thought.

The next morning when I woke, I saw Danny standing on the beach, looking serene, the tails of his open shirt blowing back from his body. I could spend my life with him; there was no question that I would be lucky to have his free spirit. I could have roots; they would have to be traveling roots, that's all. But I hoped that he was standing on the beach because he understood what I had tried to explain.

We were marrying early, to avoid the day's heat. It was before nine in the morning when Ruth closed the final button of my dress and set my flower piece on my head over my French braid. We weren't even sure the wedding would be legal anywhere else in the world, but Danny said he didn't care. 'It's real enough to me,' he had said.

'You look beautiful,' Ruth said, stepping back to take me in. I felt beautiful. 'Your mum and dad would be proud of you.'

I swallowed the lump that threatened to choke me. Ruth wasn't the sentimental type and it was even less common for her to mention my parents. It left a heavy air in the hut. Thankfully, John broke the almost sentimental moment by tapping on the door.

'Jess?'

I kissed Ruth on the cheek and moved to the door. As soon as I opened it, the look on John's face told me I would not be getting married.

13

JAKE

I wake with a dry, scratchy throat and the disgusting heaviness in my lungs that reminds me why I hardly ever smoke weed. But shoot, it was a good night. Jess and I were the last two standing. I played the guitar as she sat next to me on the two-seat sofa, pointing out star constellations and telling me stories of all her years traveling, some new, some I had heard before. I carried her to bed around four, where she curled straight into my chest and slept. I listened to her breathing slow and remember nothing more until this moment.

I slide out of her hold. She murmurs but doesn't wake. I take a quick shower and head downstairs. There's a certain bet I lost and I need to settle the score.

Downstairs in the kitchen, it doesn't seem like the others are up but the coffee machine has made a full jug. I happen to know that's Drew's timer. He has a thing for coffee machines. The more expensive, the better. He'd have had the timer set on his faithful electronic friend before any of their boxes were unpacked. You know some guys are funny about people touching their hair? Well, with Drew, you do not touch the coffee machine.

I pour myself a cup of strong coffee and an orange juice. The juice wets my throat, soothing the grit from last night. Then I set about making pancake batter. As I beat eggs, flour and milk in a large bowl, I see Brooks and Izzy on the beach, putting each other through their paces. Brooks is pinning Izzy's feet into the sand as she does sit ups; then she returns the favor. God, those two are like machines. The last thing I feel like doing is working out.

I root through the cupboards and fridge, finding sugar, lemon, maple syrup, bacon, jelly and finally, berries. My mouth stretches into a smile when I put my hand on a pack of fresh blueberries. I know exactly what I'm doing with those. Locating the apron I saw Edmond wearing on Sunday, I pull it over my head and tie the belt around my waist to protect my otherwise naked body.

I put mugs and cutlery in a pile on the table with the orange juice and jug of coffee. Then I set about grilling bacon and making pancakes, knowing the smells will draw the others soon enough. Usually, when I lose a bet, it's only Jess and I who are affected by our childish rules... meh, and sometimes Alex, but since he's half-dressed and half cut all of the time, he doesn't seem to care too much.

I hear Brooks and Izzy talking as they approach the kitchen. At the sliding doors, which I've opened onto the decking, Brooks says, 'I thought I could smell... Holy crap! Why can I see your bare ass? What are you doing?'

'Making breakfast.' I turn to him and dip my head to Izzy. 'Morning! There's coffee on the table.'

One by one, Edmond, Amelie, Kit, Madge and Marty come downstairs.

'Jesus!' Marty says. 'What the hell is wrong with you? My stomach is already tender.'

Rolling my eyes, I turn my back on him. 'You want breakfast or not?'

'Jesus, I don't know. I... yeah, I want breakfast.'

Kit puts his hands over Madge's eyes and they laugh as he walks her out to the deck.

I hear Jess talking to Becky and Drew as they near the kitchen. I smile at the last pancake in my pan. Hers.

The three of them come into the kitchen and Becky gasps as Drew shouts out, 'Want to tell me why you have no goddamn clothes on in my kitchen, kid?'

Jess squeals, startling them, and comes hurtling toward me. 'Oh my God! You lost the bet!'

We both understand the secret isn't out of the bag yet. Only Brooks and I know that Drew is going to propose this week. Well, us and now Jess. Come on, it's not like I can hide anything from her; she can read me like a basic traffic sign: quickly and easily.

I scoop her up, her legs wrapping around my waist and locking across my naked behind. 'Yeah, I guess I did.'

She pecks my cheek before I lower her to the ground and hand her a plate of bacon to carry outside. She slaps my bare ass cheek as she makes her way to the table.

I stack the pancakes I've made onto a large plate, then set the two pancakes I have made for Jess on her own plate and carry them outside.

'Dig in, guys.'

I place Jess's plate down in front of her, making sure the smile of the blueberry face I have cooked into her pancake is the right way up. Her smile disappears as she stares at it and I panic. Shit, I called this wrong. Very, very wrong.

I see her jaw tighten and her cheeks dip in as she bites down on the inside of her lip the way she does when she's trying not to cry. Shit and bigger shit. I take the empty seat beside her and tuck her wet hair behind her ear.

'I'm sorry. I'll change them. I didn't mean to upset you.'

She turns to me, her eyes full of unshed tears. 'I don't even remember telling you about this. How would you remember such a small detail as how my dad used to make my pancakes?'

'There's a very big part of me that's designated solely for Jess, babe.'

She looks at the pancakes again and lets out a big exhale. 'You're incredible, Jake Harrington.'

I press my lips to her temple. 'Eat up. They'll go cold.'

She gives me a gentle smile that doesn't fully dry her eyes. 'Okay, for being amazing, you can put some clothes on, bet or no bet.'

I twist on my chair and pour myself a coffee, finding Marty's eyes watching Jess too closely through his light glass shades.

'Nah, I think Marty kind of likes it,' I say, blowing him a kiss across the table. If he thinks I'm over the way he keeps trying to get close to her, he's got another thing coming.

'He might, but my soft furnishings don't,' Becky says, shaking her head around a mouthful of pancake. Ah, already bickering with my sister-to-be... We're a real family.

'Don't worry about it, Becky; I was checked a few weeks back. I'm clean.'

'Oh my gosh! Enough.' She balls the linen napkin from her lap and throws it across the table at me.

'Putting Jake's nakedness aside,' Sarah says, leaning forward on her elbows and taking her coffee cup in two hands, a sign her one pancake was enough for her. 'Since the boy-men are going on a fishing trip today, I took the liberty of arranging a little surprise for us ladies. I have booked us a luxurious pamper day. And the best part is, we don't even have to leave the sofa.'

'Oh, I love a pamper day,' Izzy says. 'It's been an age. My feet are ruined from dance shoes and the skin on the tips of my fingers is like granite from playing the guitar.'

Sarah purses her lips. 'Honey, that's disgusting. We'll get that fixed. We have three masseurs coming to the house. They'll do manis, pedis, whatever you like. Aaaaand... I've got bubbles!' She sings the last words as all the females around the table start up an excited conversation.

* * *

Jess was quiet through breakfast. Not obviously to other people. She smiled and joined in conversation. But I know her better than that and I'm wondering if I pushed her too far with the reminder of her childhood. That wasn't my intention. I wasn't thinking beyond doing something nice for her.

Since we're going to be apart for the day, I want to make sure she's okay before we leave the girls and head out on the water.

I tap on the bathroom door and poke my head inside. I risk a glance at her in the shower, watching water run down the arch of her back as she rinses shampoo from her hair. It's a test. I don't know whether I believe in God but I raise my eyes to the ceiling and ask him what the hell game he is trying to play with my self-restraint.

'Jess, I'm going to help pack up the truck. Come and find me when you're ready, yeah?'

'Yes. Okay. I'll be down in a few.'

As I pass Sarah's bedroom – the one she is being forced to share with Marty for the week, God help her – I see her fluffing the pillows on the bed, then folding the sheets from the sofa in the room. Huh, Marty took the sofa? That's surprisingly decent of him. I'd have thought any chance to get his arms around Sarah and he'd jump. Maybe he's not such a tool after all. I quickly change my mind. Nah, of course he is. More likely he's just conscious Sarah is Drew's legal secretary at the firm.

'Sarah, can I come in?'

'Course. What's up?'

'I want to give you this.' I hand her a roll of twenty-dollar bills. 'Please don't mention it to Jess. It's for her share of the spa thing today. If you need more, just let me know.'

Sarah takes the roll of notes I hold out to her and smiles, looking from them to me. 'I can't accept this, sweet cheeks, much as I'd love a new purse. It's all on Drew anyway.' She tucks the roll into the pocket of my jeans, then brings her hands to hold my face. 'Your momma did such a good job of raising you and Drew, you know that? I mean, you both suck when it comes to reading women. Seriously, it's like babysitting a bunch of rookies with the two of you and Brooks. But you're a true sweetheart.'

It's not often it happens, but I feel my skin heating. Instead of responding to the compliment, I tell her, 'I know women, Sarah.'

'Yeah, you all do. That's why you all mess it up so badly.' She taps my face with her fingertips. 'Lucky for you, I'm Cupid.' As she often does, Sarah turns and struts from the room, her kaftan flowing out behind her. 'Look out for my arrows, Jakey.'

The woman is a whirlwind, but one that's great to have around.

I follow her downstairs and find the voices of Drew and Edmond in the garage. The garage door is up and through it I see Kit and Brooks loading fishing gear into the back of Brooks' truck. Marty is standing at the end of the driveway on his cell phone. Honestly, I'm beginning to wonder whether there's anyone on the other end. Seems he's always on a call when there's work to be done.

'What can I do?' I ask Drew, adjusting my cap on my head.

'Put that tackle box there in the truck. We're going in that and Kit's daddymobile.'

'I heard that, man,' Kit calls from the driveway.

'Here are your sandwiches,' Becky says, coming into the garage. She hands the food to Edmond, who opens one cool box to find it full of beers, then opens another identical box to find sandwiches as well as chips and other junk.

'Pop will be pissed he missed a fishing trip,' I tell Drew as I head toward the truck.

When we were kids, we used to go fishing with Pop a couple times a year. Millie and Mom would have a girls' day and Pop, Drew and I would take off with a tent and a camp stove. It was far from extravagant, yet those were some of my best childhood memories, sitting in a small, wooden boat with my old man and my big brother, rocking to the gentle, lolling water.

While Drew was a teenager, I was only a kid, but I remember every detail. The dark green of the trees, the way my stomach would be rumbling by the time we got the stove burning and eventually managed to heat the stew Mom made for us to take. We'd lie in sleeping bags, watching the stars in the night sky, so much clearer than in the city. And we'd talk for hours, about nothing, everything.

As I load the box of tackle into the truck, I think about Jess missing out on those times with her parents. I think about how I'd like to make it up to her and force her to come on a trip like this, the kind that no kid wants to go on because it's not cool, until you're there with your old man, thinking there's nowhere else in the world you'd rather be. I want to give her that.

Right on cue, Jess comes into the garage. 'Hey, I'm ready, so what did you want to speak to me about?'

I stand, looking over the loud playsuit she is wearing. It nips in at her slim waist and emphasizes the curves of her ass and those fine breasts. Two tassels of feathers and jewels separate the two halves of the neckline. As I stand over her in her flat shoes, I glimpse enough of her cleavage to make me forget why I wanted to talk to her.

'Jake?'

I clear my throat. 'You're a five, babe. I'm not sure about the tassels. And that orange is hurting my eyes.'

She goes to hit my arm but I catch her wrist and bite the tip of her nose.

'Behave yourself. Drew, give me ten minutes?'

He nods and carries on his conversation with Edmond.

I lead Jess through the house and out to the beach by the hand. 'Sit with me.'

She mirrors my position at the edge of the water. I roll up my jeans as high as they'll go and let the water touch my bare feet.

'Wow, that's cold,' Jess says, as her toes get licked by the sea.

'How are you feeling?' I ask.

Her eyes narrow, then she says, 'A little hungover. Nothing a tough girl like me can't handle.'

'That's good, tough girl. But speaking of that tough-girl attitude, what I'm really asking is if I upset you earlier, with the pancakes?'

Her eyes widen. 'Upset me?' She sighs as she turns back out to sea. 'Oh, Jake, you can be dumb sometimes.'

Well, there's not much I can say to that. So I don't. I take a moment, enjoying the fact we can be silent and comfortable together. Also knowing that, eventually, Jess will start talking. She doesn't do silence when she's feeling emotional. It's like she thinks if she keeps moving and talking, her own thoughts can't catch her.

'My dad put blueberries in my pancakes as far back as I can remember. He used to do it for Mum too. I remember there were times he'd scrap an entire pancake because the smile didn't stay in place. And this one time, one of the blueberries popped, I guess under the heat of the pan. It was the eye of the face. And he put the pancake in front of my mum and he said, 'It's crying because you're so beautiful, it hurts.''

She smiles, a slow, steady curve of her lips. And I know she isn't with me; she's with her parents, wherever they are. She leans back on her hands, like I am, and I feel the push of sand against my own fingers where her hand comes to rest next to mine.

'I can't believe you remembered,' she says. 'I don't even recall telling you about the pancakes.' She shakes her head. 'If I wasn't too afraid to accept it, Jake, I'd say you'd be the best man I could ever ask to spend my life with.'

I replay her words in my mind. Trying to work them out, her out. Trying to control the tightness that just took over my chest and made it difficult to find my next breath.

Spend my life with Jess? I can't imagine my life any other way. Of course, I want her forever. She's Jess. My Jess. Her and me, against the world. But I can't work out that first part. *If I wasn't too afraid to accept it.* Does she wish we could be more than friends? Is she saying she'd accept someone else for the rest of her life but not me?

I can say, with certainty, I have never been as freaking confused in my life as I am this week. And usually, it would be Jess who'd talk me through a mess, make me understand the tangle of thoughts in my head. I'm afraid to push her. Yet, I need her. I need her to make sense of everything going on, the things in my head, the reason my chest feels crushed at the thought of her spending her life with anyone other than me. Knowing that, like with Emily, that could be a real possibility one day.

'What are you afraid of, Jess?'

She glances at me and looks away just as quickly, as if she's contemplating her next words. 'I'm afraid that...'

'Afraid that what?'

She pulls her knees up to her chest and wraps her arms around them, still not meeting my eye. 'I'm afraid that... that you could be... that you could be what my dad was to my mum.' She closes her eyes. 'That you could be my fatal attraction. That you could be the person I can't live without. The person who ends me. I think I'm afraid of you, Jake.

The way... The things I feel here, with you, your family, Emily. I'm terrified of it all.'

I can't tell you why my eyes start to sting. Why I feel like, for the first time since I was a kid, I could cry. I know how hard those words must have been for her. And it hasn't occurred to me that... fuck, she could love me the way her mum loved her dad?

The lump that builds in my throat makes it hard to breathe. And though I try to swallow it away, it won't go.

'You let go of the fear once,' I tell her.

Her *pfft* of laughter, short and somber, doesn't shift the heavy air around us. 'Yeah, look how well that turned out.'

'Jess, you were nineteen when you and Danny planned to marry. You can't cling to that failure forever. Don't hold on to it for so long you let it ruin your future relationships.'

My voice falters as it occurs to me that I'm not sure whether I'm talking about our relationship or relationships with other people.

'That's a little ironic coming from you, wouldn't you say? You were a kid when you fell in love with Emily and you're still blinded by it.' Her voice shifts; there's an undertone of something that's possibly anger.

Love Emily? Yeah, I do. I did. But I've never felt anything like I just felt when Jess called me the person she can't live without.

'No. I always loved Emily but not... not like that. I wasn't in love.'

I'm only realizing now how true that statement is.

Jess finally looks at me. 'So when? How did you know that she wasn't only your best friend and you wanted more?'

I search the horizon, as if I'll find the answer there. 'I don't know. I guess, the end of college. I was about to leave and she still had two years to go. It was going to be the first time since we were babies that we wouldn't be together. It's not like it happened overnight. I don't ever remember suddenly wanting to rip her clothes off or anything.'

Not like with Jess.

I stare at her, at the wisps that have come free from her hair tie and blow around her perfect skin, around those big, brown eyes.

'Have you ever thought that... maybe you were just scared to lose her? Maybe she and Brandon are the right couple?'

She swings my thoughts right back to that jackass and how much I'd like to punch him in the gut.

'Jake! You ready?' We turn to see Drew standing by the pool, shouting down to us.

I lift my cap from my head as if to say, *I heard you. I'm coming.*

I stand and offer a hand to Jess.

'Jake, as your friend, I think maybe it's time you made up with Emily. Let sleeping dogs lie and all that. Don't ruin what you guys shared because she fell for a jerk instead of you.'

'I'll think about that, Yoda.' I place my cap on her head and lift her chin. 'Maybe you should think about whether your parents would have rather loved and lost than never experienced the time they had here together.'

'You think the risk was worth it, huh?'

'You tell me.'

I steal my cap back and press my lips to her forehead. 'I've got to go.'

She nods and folds her arms across her chest. 'Have a good day fishing. I can't imagine anything worse.'

'That's why you're not invited,' I call back over my shoulder. 'Enjoy painting the world pink.'

'Bring me back a tiny fish that is so small, we can't even cook it up.'

'Save me some cucumber face mask. You know how I love utterly pointless shit.'

I hear her laugh as I make my way up to the deck.

14

JAKE

I've missed getting out on the water. Being brought up on Staten Island by a man who loved to fish, Drew and I were both taught how to captain a boat. But this is his week, so I'm playing designated driver so he can have a few beers with the others. Plus, I've been itching to put this bad-boy boat into full throttle.

Water sprays from the sides of the bow and wind blows in my face as I steer us into the open ocean. The guys have cracked their first beers. Kit, Drew and Brooks stand by the cockpit, joking around. Edmond and Marty are sitting on the padded seats at the bow. Our gear is in bags on the deck at the back of the boat.

The ultimate big-kid playground.

I crank the sound system loud enough to hear the rock tunes over the sound of the engines driving us forward. It's a calm day, the chop is low, and we make good time out to the spot we've decided to fish.

I bring us to a stop around forty minutes from shore. Drew stands on the bow – brother team – directing me to a spot where he can drop anchor. The others grab a second beer and Brooks throws me a club soda. As we unpack and set up the gear, Marty takes a suspiciously timed call, doing nothing to help.

Edmond, being the one most happy handling bait, hooks up live bait to the rods and we take turns to cast into the water. I set my rod in its holster and sit on the edge of the boat. The clouds clear, opening up the sky to sunlight. The kind that appears to spray beams as it cascades toward the sea and illuminates the surface. I close my eyes and lean back, feeling the warmth on my face. And I remember something Jess once said to me.

'I see my parents every day,' she said. 'I see them in the blue of the sea, the green of the grass. I hear them in the song of birds and the whistle of the wind. I see them in the beams that shine around the sun, as if they're lighting up the sky to say hello. And I feel like they're always here, always watching me from another time and place.'

Out here, on the open ocean, feeling insignificant in comparison to the world, I think maybe she's right. Somewhere, out there, they are watching her. They're taking care of her from afar. Coexisting with us, in another form.

Only Jess could make me see something like that. Only Jess could make me see how small we all are in the grand scheme of life.

I silently thank her folks, wherever they are, for sending her to me, or allowing her to stay with me. I thank them for watching over her and for giving her the strength to have come through everything in her life and still be incredible.

And I tell them that I wish I had known them. I can only imagine the kind of people they were. But I do know they must have had greatness in them because Jess has it now.

'You sure you don't want a beer, Jakey?' Brooks asks, pulling me from my own thoughts.

'I'm good, buddy. You guys go ahead and get wasted.'

Marty takes a bottle from Brooks' hand and holds it up in my direction. 'If you say so.'

I turn to Kit, who is sitting on a padded seat at the back of the boat, next to me. 'Has he always been this arrogant?'

'Ah, yes, always. But I think maybe you're a little sensitive to it this trip,' Kit says.

'It's a wonder no one has socked him in the face yet.'

'Oh, they have,' Drew says, heading over. 'When we were associates at the firm, Marty got too close to another guy's girl and he paid for it with a purple shiner.'

I shake my head. 'Yeah, I can believe that,' I say, glaring down the boat at Marty's back.

'Although I do agree with Kit,' he adds. 'Maybe because Marty has showed Jess some attention, you're being a bit tetchy.'

'A *bit* of attention? He's been giving her fuck-me eyes since we arrived.'

'All right, I'm lost,' Kit says to me. 'I thought you were trying to get Emily back? What am I missing?'

I contemplate telling him about Emily. Our saga. But I can't be bothered.

I realize I've run out of steam on the whole Emily thing. I'd like her back in my life but... that's all. I half smile and let out a short laugh as I realize: I'm over it. I'm over Emily. Maybe I should never have thought about changing our relationship. Then I never would have lost her.

That doesn't mean I'm over the lies. It just means I know I don't want to be with her like that. Maybe Jess was right. Maybe I couldn't stand the thought of losing Ems, and being in love with her was the only way I could think to keep her in my life.

The squeal of a line steals all our attention.

'You're on, Jakey!' Brooks calls.

I jump into action, flicking off my cap and taking control of my rod as whatever has taken my bait pulls the line far out to sea. I let it go until it calms, then I slow the reel and try to control the fish. Slowly, cautiously, I work the line, encouraging my catch back toward the boat.

'She's heavy,' I say, tugging back on the rod.

'Congratulations, you finally caught something you wanted.'

I turn to where Marty is standing, leaning on the screen of the cockpit, chugging on a thick cigar, his shades in place, his hair slicked to one side.

'Yeah, no thanks to you,' I snarl.

'Concentrate, Jake. This could be dinner,' Edmond says.

I try to focus on the fish and line. But Marty comes closer. 'Are we still talking about the fish on your line or are we talking about the girl you're too pussy to admit you're into?'

'Is he fucking kidding me?' I ask, looking at Drew, knowing these guys are colleagues and for my brother's sake, I probably shouldn't break Marty's jaw. 'I know you didn't call me a pussy, man.'

This time, I glare at Marty.

'Ah, come on. You're like a brooding teen. *Emily, I want you. No, Jess, I want you. Someone please want me.*' He shakes his head and puffs on his cigar again.

I start to see red.

'Shut the fuck up, Marty. And stay the hell away from Jess.'

The boat falls silent, other than the sound of Edmond taking the rod from me as I rise to full height, facing Marty, willing myself to exercise some self-control. Knowing, if he keeps it up, one of us is going to wind up in the sea.

'Why? Shouldn't someone make use of her since you seem to have lost your balls?'

I close my eyes, trying to force away my desire to put my fist in his face. It doesn't work. I open my eyes and all I can see is him and how much I want to hit him.

'Jake.' I hear Drew's warning tone as I charge.

I drop my shoulder into Marty's gut and propel him back, hard. Hard enough to take us both overboard.

We plummet into the cold water. I open my eyes to make sure he's okay, for some goddamn reason, then I kick up to the surface.

He breaks the water after me, coughing and spluttering.

'Have you lost your goddamn mind?'

'I told you not to fucking push me.'

'Christ, Jake. If you're this nuts over her, do something about it.'

'You think I don't fucking want to, Marty? Huh?' I run a hand through my wet hair, pushing it back from my face as my legs tread the ocean. 'There have to be two people to make a relationship, you asshole.'

'You don't say.' He laughs. 'Look, all I can tell you is, every time I've spoken to her, she talks about you. Every godforsaken word that leaves her mouth is some variation of how great you are, even when she doesn't realize she's doing it.'

I stare at him, both of us doggy paddling. It is? 'She's crazy about you, Jake, whether she wants to accept it or not. Maybe if you took your head out of your ass long enough, you'd both see that you're perfect for each other. You don't want other men to have her? Do it yourself.'

He swims the few yards back to the boat and Drew glares at me as he gives Marty a hand up.

I can hear Marty say, 'I thought *you* were crazy over Becky. Your brother takes it to a new level.'

I take a deep breath and sink into the water, exhaling, trying to find the answer to what the hell I'm supposed to do from here.

If what Marty says is true, if she feels like that, and she still won't take down her walls, how can we keep going on? I can't be the person who makes her afraid every day. But if I push, if I force her to take my hand and break down those walls with me, I have to be sure. Or I lose her. I'll lose her like I lost Emily.

But the way the thought of losing Jess wrecks my body, makes my heart feel like it would rather stop beating than be without her, I know what I have to do.

I kick up to the surface and get back on the boat.

'That was a two-hundred-dollar cigar you ruined, jackass,' Marty says.

'Just thinking of your lungs, man.'

'Crazy mother...'

* * *

We dock the boat, Drew and Brooks tying off the lines as I steer. We unload and then split into the two cars. Still wet from my dip in the ocean, I sit on a towel in the passenger seat of Brooks' truck. He and Kit talk across the seats but I don't hear anything. I haven't heard much since my run-in with Marty. All I've felt is the increasing tightness in my gut. All I've seen is Jess. The way she looks at me. And I wonder why I never saw it before.

By the time we get back to the house, I'm a pent-up ball of emotion.

Brooks pats my back when he, Kit and I stand on the driveway at the back of the truck. 'Go do what you've got to do, man. We've got this.'

I take an unsteady breath. Where do I even start?

Patting his arm, I move past him. 'Thanks.'

As I walk through the house, I hear the girls talking and laughing. I kick off my wet sneakers and follow the voices out to the deck. The girls are sitting around, drinking champagne. I notice Emily there too and I feel her eyes on me, but I haven't got time for her. Only Jess.

The voices stop as I step onto the deck and look her way. She smiles. The kind of smile that somehow steadies my nerves when I'm not sure anything else can. I'm vaguely aware of Sarah asking why my clothes are wet, but I can only focus on the stunning woman, my best friend, who is staring back at me.

Jess sits forward, placing her glass down on the table before her, reading me like only she can, knowing I need her. 'Is everything okay?' she asks.

I think I shake my head as I tell her, 'No.' The word comes out barely more than a whisper, croaking through my dry throat.

She stands and comes over to me, concern on her face. She runs her hands down my arms, leaving goosebumps in their wake.

'What's wrong, Jake? You're worrying me.'

I want to tuck her hair behind her ear. I want to run my thumbs across the smooth skin of her cheeks. I want to kiss the lips I can't take my eyes from.

But not here. Not like this.

I slip my hand into hers and lead her through the house, up the stairs to our bedroom. I set my cell phone to play our playlist. One we made months ago called 'Friday Nights with Red Wine'.

She stands in front of the closed door, not coming closer to me. I open the doors of the bedroom balcony, letting the sea breeze blow into the room and the fresh salt air surround us. Then I cross the room to her.

'Jake?'

I didn't know until now what I wanted, what I needed to do. Now, staring at her lips and the eyes that can make me lose myself, I know that what I need is to make love to her. Regardless of the consequences or what happens next.

I step in to her, forcing her back against the bedroom door. I stare into her deep brown eyes as I take hold of her face and trace her features with my thumbs. Her closed eyelids, the outline of her nose, the shape of her lips.

'Jake,' she whispers.

I know, in that word, she's afraid. I'm inside her walls.

Yeah, well, she's inside mine too. And I'm afraid. I'm afraid of this ruining everything. I'm afraid of losing her. But I'm more afraid of never making love to her, bigger and more meaningful than when we've been together before. Of never making love to a woman I am truly, unequivocally, in love with.

'Shh.' I press my lips to her left eyelid, then her right. She sighs as I tip her head back and bring my mouth to the skin of her neck, inhaling the scent of lemongrass from her spa day.

I take in every crease of her soft, pink lips before I cover them with mine. I part them with my tongue, savoring the taste of her, mixed with champagne, and delight in her groan.

I kiss her here, gently, tentatively, until her hands rise from her sides and she takes hold of my T-shirt, fisting it at my hips. She finally opens her eyes and I see they are full of unshed tears. The sight makes my chest tight. Is she feeling this too? God, I hope so.

I hope I haven't called this wrong. And I pray we can get through her defenses. Because I need her. I need her to be more than the person who makes me laugh and smile. More than the person I depend on and who I want to be able to depend on me.

'You're beautiful, Jess.'

And I mean more than the way she looks. I'm talking about her soul. The way the shape of her fits the shape of me like we are supposed to be together. I see it now.

And I'm wondering why the hell I ever fought it. All because of Emily? It seems crazy now that feeling hurt and betrayed could have kept me away from Jess.

I close my eyes and pull back from her, resting a hand on the door above her head, steadying myself as the enormity of what I'm hearing in my own mind, what I'm feeling in every cell of my body, hits me.

She needs to be able to depend on me the way I know I can her. I'm here, forcing her to face her fears, and hoping to hell she can, for both of us. But maybe I'm pushing too hard, too fast.

'I'm sorry,' I say, keeping my eyes closed, trying to calm my racing heart. Begging her to fight through those fears.

When I open my eyes, hers are locked on mine. Her chest rises and falls with her deep breaths. Her lips part and she looks at me as if she's taking in everything about me.

'Kiss me, Jess. I won't push you. I'm asking you. You're in my head. You've been in my head every moment since I met you. So kiss me.'

She doesn't move for what feels like a lifetime. I think she stops breathing. And my hope, my faith, falls away.

At least I tried. I put myself out there. And she doesn't—

She clasps her hands around my nape and pulls my mouth back to hers. I take her hands above her head, pinning her to the door with my entire body. Craving her touch, all of her.

As the words of our songs drift into the room, I see images of us: laughing in bars, dancing, watching movies together, crashing a canoe in Hyde Park, rolling on sand, in the sea. For the first time, I'm not afraid. We have a past together, she is truly my female counterpart, and this makes me want her more.

It makes me want us. We're perfect for each other. It's blindingly obvious now.

I roll my hips against her as she presses her lips to my neck. 'You taste salty,' she whispers against my lobe.

'I had a run in with the ocean.'

She pulls back and bites her lip, stopping her smile from spreading to her cheeks. But that move doesn't distract me; it only makes my insatiable need deeper.

I'm lost to us. To her. And I don't want to be anywhere else. I don't want to think of anything else. I want to drown in her. I want her to bowl me over with her waves, hurtling me into a spin, taking me over, the way I know she can. She can have all of me.

I pull her lip from her teeth and nip it in my own, running my hands over her body, just not able to get enough of her.

She flips my cap to the ground and tugs on my hair as she kisses me back, showing me she wants me as much as I want her.

'Jess, I'm... I...'

Don't, Jake. Don't say it. Don't make her run.

She stops, shaking her head, seeming happy for me to keep those three words to myself, no matter how much I mean them. No matter how much I want her to move beyond her past and have faith in her future. Have faith in me.

'No. Jake. I can't.'

My heart starts hammering in my chest for the wrong reason. My entire torso feels like it's dropped to the floor.

'Jess, stop overthinking. Do what feels right.'

Please. Please trust me.

'I just... I can't.' She steps out of my hold. Whether it's the loss of contact or that I'm topless in the breeze coming through the window, I'm suddenly cold. 'What if...? I think... are you even drunk?'

Her question is like a thousand razor blades slicing my flesh at once.

'Drunk?'

So, this is the same as normal to her? No. I won't accept that. I know it's more. I pray it's more.

'Well, are you? I mean, that's the rule.'

The way she looks at her feet tells me she wasn't thinking about the rules a moment ago.

She rubs a hand across her lips and steps past me, moving to the window, leaving me staring at nothing but a closed door.

Have you ever felt like you're at a crossroads? Like the decision to turn left, or right, or to drive straight over could set your life on an entirely different course? You know each path could be dangerous. It could be the wrong way to go. But somehow, one of those roads speaks to you. It beckons you in and dares you to take it.

I could be taking the wrong road. I could be setting us both on a cataclysmic course.

But damn it, I'm doing it anyway.

I cross the room and step behind her as she looks out to sea. I press my chest to her back and rest my chin on her shoulder.

'I'm not drunk, Jess. I'm as sober as I've ever been. And I've never been thinking more clearly than I am in this moment.'

I kiss her neck until she rolls her head back and covers my arms with her own.

It's the slightest move of her head but it comes. She nods. I waste no time in taking her away from her thoughts. I turn her to me. She holds my face as she kisses me, agreeing to let me take her far away from this room, far away from her fears, if only for now.

15

JESS

When the airplane hit the tarmac at London Heathrow, the bounce of the wheels woke me from a deep sleep. It was a little more than two years ago and I can still remember standing on the top step of the plane, rain blowing against my face, the cold of England striking my body, which was more used to warm climates. I remember how I just stood there, still, looking at the gray sky, breathing in the less than fresh air, thinking how I immediately felt more at home here than I had in the last fifteen years.

I collected my backpack and, tired as I was from my night flight from Los Angeles, I rode the Tube as far west as I could go. Then I took another train over ground and then a bus. It's remarkable, in some ways, that I even knew how to get there. In other ways, I could never have forgotten how to find my childhood home.

I hoisted my backpack on tighter and walked the few hundred meters to the street I grew up on. I had decided months before that I needed to come back. I had started to forget those magical days, the sights, the smells, the green of the trees that lined the street. I had sometimes thought about returning before and I suppose I was afraid that doing so would ruin the memories I had, which I held on a pedestal. That instead of seeing lush green and bright blue skies, instead of hearing the laughter of children playing in the street, I would see a damp, gray, lifeless street. More than that, I feared I wouldn't see their faces any more. That the blush of my mum's cheeks, the brightness of my dad's eyes, would have been replaced by memories of him sick in his bedroom. That I would remember the day my mum and I moved out because she couldn't bear to be where they had once been incredibly happy.

But I sat on the red brick wall of the front garden opposite my old home and looked at the once blue door, now white. And it came back. Tears filled my eyes as I saw my dad playing with me on the lawn. Despite the drizzling rain coming down on me, I could see the blue skies and I saw my mum bringing ice-lollies out to Dad and me because it was so hot.

I sat on the wall for hours, smiling, until an elderly lady came out of her house nearby. My eyes squinted as I took in her vaguely familiar face.

'Can I help you, dear?' she asked. She didn't shoo me away or ask why someone who probably looked homeless was sitting on her wall.

'Mrs Ashley?' I asked.

She looked at me, scrutinizingly, the way I suspected I was looking at her. 'I'm sorry, I don't...' Then she gasped. 'Jessica?'

I nodded too quickly. 'Yes. Yes, it's Jess.'

She surprised me, wrapping her arms around me in a hug, and a bizarre sense of homeliness came over me as I breathed in her scent, still powdery like baby talc and floral perfume.

She invited me into her house and asked me my story as we drank tea and ate old English biscuits. We talked long into the afternoon, until her front door burst open and giggling voices came into the kitchen. Mrs Ashley's grandchildren crashed into her stomach, the girl, then the boy.

I smiled as she asked about their day at school and they told her tiny, pointless details about snapped crayons and broken biscuits at reading time, but she was interested.

'Oh, hello.'

I turned to see a woman I instantly recognized.

'Stephanie Ashley! Hi! It's Jess. I used to live—'

'Oh my gosh, yes! I remember you lived across the road. We went to school together.'

Like her mother did, she hugged me. It was one of the most bizarre days of my adult life, and there had been a few. As we spoke of our past and Mrs Ashley told us stories we didn't even remember, I had an overwhelming sense of belonging. For the first time ever, it felt as if I had a past. Not one that I had made up and perhaps even twisted, but one that other people had shared.

I stayed with Mrs Ashley for a few weeks. I helped her by doing chores around her house and she came with me some days to buy materials and fastenings for my clothes. I hadn't intended to stay in the UK. I wasn't sure where I was headed; I had only wanted to come and refresh my memory of my parents, but in those weeks, I found myself reluctant to leave. And so, for the first time since I could remember, I considered planting roots.

Small roots, that could be dug up easily and carried with me, but semi-permanent roots, nonetheless.

I spent time in London, trying to get my clothes into boutique stores. I found one taker in Camden Market and one store on Portobello Road. Both were known for their slightly alternative clothing and given the Asian twist I put on most of my pieces, I thought the fit was perfect. I wrote a few articles and submitted them to magazines. Eventually, one fashion magazine offered me the role of writing semi-regular articles on alternative fashion and international clothing inspiration, for a small sum. Since I had a lot of photographs from traveling, it worked out well.

I had income, but I knew I could take either job anywhere with me. I could submit articles via email and I could have my clothes shipped from almost any place on earth. I had no idea where I would go next but I could flee if I wanted to. The thought of staying in one spot was something I didn't think I could manage any more. It was all I knew, moving on. For so long, I had wanted to feel like I belonged somewhere, but I had traveled alone for so many years, my longest relationships lasting only weeks, I knew I would end up running at some point. I needed an out when things became too much.

My clothes slowly began to sell in the two stores, until I had them in four stores, and I needed to look for a studio space. I was also conscious that I needed to leave Mrs Ashley's home, having probably overstayed my welcome.

The lady who owned the Camden Market boutique put me in touch with Jenni, who owned a studio in Camden. It was the third floor of a building, above one of Camden's many sex shops. As you can imagine, I wasn't feeling it initially, but I climbed the rickety staircase anyway and knocked on the white door of the studio.

'Come in! Come in!'

I couldn't place the source of the voice but figured the call was to me, so I pushed inside, surprised to find a huge, white, open space filled with canvasses on easels, paints, materials. A radio was playing Sheryl Crow's 'All I Wanna Do.'

I took in the artsy space, thinking I could definitely work there. Then I was practically knocked off my feet by a girl with pixie hair wearing jean shorts and a polka-dot T-shirt. She bumped her hip into mine with such force, I rocked to the side and reached out to the wall to support myself.

'You must be Jess.'

As I took in all her ear piercings, her nose ring and lip stud, and the tattoo sleeve inked on her left arm, I confirmed I was.

'Well, take a look around. I lost the guy I shared with last week – he moved to a bigger space – and I could use someone straight in to split the cost.'

She moved around the space quickly as she spoke, disorienting me. She disappeared behind a door into another room, which I assumed was a toilet until she left the door open and kept talking, then I figured it couldn't be. After I'd started working there, I realized Jenni had actually been talking to me from the toilet. She was quite a free spirit like that.

'Have you eaten lunch?' she asked.

I moved to a modern painting of a woman's face on the wall, taking in the bright colors. 'Erm, no, actually.'

Jenni reappeared. 'Great. Let's go to the market.'

It was a sunny day in Camden. We ate chickpea curry outside, sat on old whisky barrels as we shared one, then two, bottles of wine, the alcohol cementing our friendship.

'So, you'll take the space?' Jenni asked, once the wine fog had already taken hold.

'What would the arrangement be?'

'Six months. Pay me two weekly. We'll split the room down the middle. Simple.'

I took a gulp of wine, then set my glass down on the barrel. 'Six months?'

'O-oh, I've got you sussed. You're one of those, aren't you?'

'One of those what?' I asked.

She shrugged as she drained the last of the wine directly from the bottle. 'A commitment-phobe.'

'I am not a commitment-phobe.' I pondered that. 'I've just never had to commit to anything before now.'

'Mm hm. Gotcha. Well, think it over. I have someone else looking at the place tomorrow and I can't afford to pass up any offers, but I'd like you to take it. I can already tell we're going to be good friends.'

She said it so seriously, as if it genuinely didn't matter whether I chose to be her friend or not. I started to laugh and something took hold of me: wine, fear, the oddness of having been in the UK for the last few weeks. It kept my laughter coming until my sides hurt. It felt too good to stop.

I stayed with Jenni that night, taking her sofa. I was going to leave in the morning without waking her. If her head felt as groggy as mine was, I figured she'd be thankful. But she caught me as I was folding up the duvet she'd loaned me.

'When you accept my offer, I'm thinking you'll need a place to live?' She padded through the lounge and into the kitchen to boil the kettle.

'I told you, Jenni, I need to think about it.'

'Okay. But, when you do accept, I know a couple of guys who are looking for someone to take their third room. It's small but a good price. Do you want a bagel?'

I was going to say no but my stomach growled at me, and I thought maybe it would alleviate some of the sick feeling I had inside, so I said yes.

I still wasn't sure I could commit to being in London for six months. In fact, my gut was telling me to turn the place down, but I took the number of the apartment Jenni gave me and I texted some guy called Jake to see if I could view the spare room.

* * *

When I arrived at the door of the apartment, the top floor of a split house in west London, I double checked the number and knocked. Seconds later, the door was flung open and a man, naked but for his boxers, was standing in front of me.

'Jesus,' I said, recoiling.

'All right?'

The naked man winked at me, then his hand went to his boxers as he shuffled his piece. I almost ran right then. No way in hell was I staying in this place with this pervert.

'I'm Alex,' he said, holding out a hand.

I considered his hand, then his tall, slim, pale body. 'You just touched yourself and now you're asking me to shake your hand?'

He laughed and scrutinized me, head to toe, from my heeled boots and skinny jeans to my leather jacket and my hair pulled across my shoulder.

'She's got my vote, Jake,' he said, leaving me in the doorway.

I stepped inside for some unknown reason.

'It's been fun, kids,' I could hear someone say, 'but I've got to go. Someone is here to view the spare room and Alex is naked.'

'Alex is always naked,' a second voice said. 'Okay, son, be safe. We love you.'

'Love you too, Mom.'

I leaned farther into the lounge and saw the source of the voice, a man standing in the kitchen, talking into a laptop that was on the kitchen counter. The first thing that struck me was that his voice was deep and smooth. The second thing was it had an American accent.

'See you, baby brother,' a new female voice said.

'Bye, Mill. Take care of my niece and nephew.'

'Catch you later, jackass.' Those words came from a man and they made Jake smile, a smile which pulled on only half of his mouth and caused a dimple in his cheek.

'Fuck off, dickhead.' He closed the lid of the laptop, then lifted his head so I could finally see his full face under the peak of his black cap. And, damn, did it hit me full force. That smile wasn't all he had going for him. Dark stubble lined a sharp jaw – not too sharp, just perfectly sharp.

His dark eyes narrowed on me as he stared without moving. Something leaped inside me. It jumped from my stomach to under my breastbone and made me close my eyes for a moment.

'Hi, I'm Jake.'

As he stepped from behind the counter, giving me the full view of his broad, muscular body under his fitted white T-shirt and dark jeans, I swallowed to wet my dry throat.

'Jess.'

He lifted his cap and scratched his head of thick, brown hair. 'Sorry about my roommate. He has like a birth defect or something.'

I smiled. 'Yeah, I figured there was something going on there.'

He replaced his cap and leaned his head to one side. 'That's an English accent with a difference.'

'Mm, yeah, well, I've lived a lot of places.'

And nowhere.

His eyes never left mine, as if he was waiting for more information, but I didn't give it. This wasn't going to be a long-term arrangement, even if I did decide to stay. I didn't need to share things with him.

He let out a short *pfft* of laughter. 'All right then, Jess from Nowhere and Everywhere, let me show you around.'

I watched his back muscles move beneath his T-shirt as I followed him through the lounge-kitchen-diner area, along a corridor and to my potential bedroom. It wasn't much, completely empty but for a wardrobe and a mattress-less double bed. But it was better than most places I'd stayed in the last fifteen years. Plus, it had an en suite. I could be alone here as much as I wanted.

As we stepped back into the hallway, Alex came out of his bedroom, still almost naked, but now smelling of aftershave.

'Christ man, put some clothes on,' Jake said, the break in his voice betraying his amusement.

Alex shrugged. 'She needs to know what she's getting herself into if she lives here. Jess, my love, I don't do clothes in the house. I do women. Lots of women. If you want...'

He winked at me again.

'While that's a delightful offer, and, might I add, very politely put, it's Sunday, day of rest and all,' I said.

Jake laughed hard, with his head thrown back and the skin of his neck pulled taut across his Adam's apple. Damn, the man was sexy as hell.

'I like her,' Alex said. 'Let's keep her.' Then he was gone from the corridor.

Jake led me to the kitchen and pulled out a stool for me. 'Grab a seat. Beer?'

I was about to object but he was already taking two bottles from the fridge. 'Looks like I don't have much choice.'

'Things you need to know,' he said, unhooking the lids from the bottles. 'Alex doesn't wear enough clothes, and he really is frisky but harmless. For my part, you should never refuse beer, wings or burgers and we'll get along just fine.'

He handed a bottle of beer to me and I watched him swig from his own. My lips curled up and I still have no idea why. I just... liked him. When I realized I was staring, I dragged my eyes away, looking for anything to distract me. My focus landed on his laptop.

'Were you on a video call before?' I asked, stating the obvious.

'Yeah, it's a family thing. Probably something else you should know about me. I Skype my family a lot. I'm a big family guy – even my closest friends are family.'

I took a gulp of beer and played with the label on the bottle, a wave of unexplainable emotion floating over me.

'Sorry, does that make you think I'm weird or something?' he asked.

'Weird? God, no.' Then I don't know what came over me, but I told this hot stranger, 'I guess, if anything, it makes me feel envious.'

I didn't know why I said it and I didn't want him to push me any further. My chest fluttered with panic as he questioned me with a look.

He stepped back against the kitchen counter and folded his bulging biceps across his toned pecs. I remember thinking, *Hell, I do have a libido.*

'So, Mysterious Jess, do you want the place?'

I took a deep breath and sat up straighter on my stool. 'The lease is six months?'

He nodded. 'Unless you want to sign up for longer. I'm sure the landlord—'

'Oh, God, longer would definitely not be necessary. I don't really hang around. Six months would be the longest I've stayed anywhere since... for a long time.'

'Well, what do you say to six months?'

I wanted to say no. Something about this man set my alarm bells ringing. A sexy as sin man who valued family and friends, who wasn't ready to flee to some remote part of the world next week. I wanted to run. Yet, the word that left my mouth was, 'Okay.'

That delectable smile curved on one side of his lips again. 'I'll have a word with Alex about wearing more clothes.'

'I'd appreciate that.'

The next day, I signed a lease and Jake took me shopping for furniture. We spent night after night building flat pack things for my room. After that, when I made my own soft furnishings, I made him some too. I had a home. I had a friend. I had things to call my own. For the first time since my mum died, I had a bed that I actually owned.

When my six months were up, I signed for another six, and another six, and another. My small roots grew deep into London, deep into Jake, deep into a version of me I had wanted since I was an orphaned girl. Jake became my roots and he became my best friend. I told him about my life and he told me everything about his. We picked each other up when we were down. We cared for each other when we were sick. And he became the wind that blew just enough between my branches to keep life interesting. I had roots and leaves. I was a complete tree. And I started to feel again. I let myself feel just enough to remind myself I was human.

Jake became the most precious thing in the world to me and I would never, will never, risk losing him.

16

JAKE

The alarm on my cell phone vibrates but I catch it quickly, since I've hardly slept. Jess is tucked under my arm, her head resting on my chest, where she's been since the third time we made love last night. She looks so peaceful, I don't want to wake her.

I take her in for a few more minutes, listening to the song of the waves through the open bedroom window. The black of the night is beginning to turn to a dark shade of blue as the moon begins to make way for the sun.

I've been here, laying still for hours, trying not to wake Jess, as my mind exploded with too many thoughts to get a handle on any. I said we made love. And we did. There's no question. The way she looked into my soul as we moved together, the way the universe seemed to shrink until it was only us, in our moment. Or, perhaps our moment felt as large as the universe.

The thing is, if I felt it, she must have felt it too. Maybe not as hard and powerful. Maybe it didn't consume her completely. But she must have felt the shift between us. We weren't two friends treating each other to the best time any person could give another. We were more than that, so much more. The playfulness that is usually between us, the frantic heat, they were replaced with what felt like lightning bolts coming from my heart to hers. She was part of me. I was part of her. We were two halves of a whole.

And if she felt it, her instinct will tell her to run. That's who Jess is. She's a runner. Living with me in London is the longest she's stayed in one place in her entire adult life. As I lay in bed, I wondered why. Why had she chosen to stay in London? Chosen to stay anywhere, finally? I questioned why we ever started sleeping together. And I wondered how much champagne she had yesterday, whether, when she woke in a panic, she would use it as an excuse.

So, when I heard the others come back from the pub around one in the morning, I slipped out of Jess's hold and I went to Brooks' room to put a plan in motion.

The plan is simply this: distract her long enough to get her over the initial panic. Then, I've no damn clue. But I know, if she wakes and starts thinking about whether she could have stronger feelings for me than friendship, she'll think about her parents. She'll think about her fear of falling in love. Of loving someone so much, it can bring an end to everything.

'Jess. Babe, wake up.' I stroke her cheek and press my lips to her hair. My heart bursts when she rubs a knuckle into her eye and lifts her head, completely disoriented.

'What's wrong? What time is it?'

She glances down at my chest and I see a subtle shift in her eyes, as if the realization that she slept with me in every sense of the word and she wasn't wasted dawns on her. It's the confirmation I need. I'm making the right decision here, even if it involves forcing her to rise at four in the morning.

Before she has a chance to think or say another word, I lift her to sit and talk-whisper instructions, trying not to wake anyone else in the house. 'You need to get up; I'm taking you somewhere.'

'But. What?'

I can't resist. I lean on the bed and steal a kiss. 'You are insanely adorable when you're sleepy.' I take her hand and tug her from the bed. 'Up. Now. Put swimwear under your clothes.'

She stands on the spot, staring at me.

I clap my hands. 'Babe, let's go, let's go. Chop-chop.'

'What the...?' She drops her hands to her hips. 'I know you did not clap your hands at me.'

'Finally, she's awake. Get to it.'

I leave her tutting as I make quick work of cleaning my teeth. She comes into the bathroom, wearing only a bikini, and I greedily take her in. How in God's name did I resist her for so damn long?

She puts paste on her brush and scowls at me as she cleans her teeth next to me. I spit. She spits. Then she slips her feet into sandals as I pull on sneakers.

I grab the keys to Brooks' truck from the drawer where I left them after talking with him a few hours ago, and I lead Jess outside.

'What are we doing?' she asks again as she climbs into the truck.

I turn the keys in the ignition but before I pull out of the driveway, I turn to her. 'I want to start the day with you. I want to spend every second of today with you. Just us. From beginning to end. Is that all right?'

She doesn't say anything as she looks deep into my eyes. That panic is there, lingering beneath the surface. I know her. I know every subtle expression she makes. I know that her mind is screaming at her to run. I try to tell her in a look that she's going to have me to contend with before she can even make a move.

I sit, not speaking, until there's the slightest incline of her head and she croaks, 'Okay.'

I lower the windows and head out to the beach. The sky lightens as we drive. Jess slips off her sandals and pulls her bare legs up to the seat, her denim shorts not covering much of those fine legs at all. As we drive, the only car on the road, the wind blows her hair back and she rests her chin on her hand, her elbow on the window ledge, staring out to sea. If someone asked me to take a picture of perfection, I would take her in this moment. And I would call it *The Weight of the World*.

I understand her confusion. Hell, I feel it too. And I know her fears. Right now, they're becoming mine, because if she runs, I think she'll take a part of me with her. I can't risk that. I have to take it easy. Even if she won't accept my love, I have to keep her in my life, however she'll have me.

I cover the hand resting on her thigh and I squeeze. 'Stop overthinking, Jess. Let's just enjoy today. It's you, and me, an open road and a beach.'

She doesn't look at me but she squeezes my hand as she continues to gaze out of the window. I'll take it.

Right before the beach I've chosen, I see an open café. I swing the truck into the parking lot and make quick work of picking up two drinks. A coconut latte for Jess and a black coffee for me.

'Take these?' I ask, sliding into the truck.

'Mm, caffeine,' she says, inhaling through the small hole in the top of the lid.

'Aaaand...' I hand her the brown paper bag that holds her favorite: cinnamon rolls. Finally, I get a smile. 'If I'd known a cinnamon roll was all it would take to cure Little Miss Grumpy I would have driven faster.'

She scowls playfully. 'Shut up. Any woman would be grouchy if you woke her up at four in the morning.'

'But I wouldn't buy cinnamon swirls for just any woman.'

'No, I suppose you wouldn't.' She laughs, a tiny, short sound. But it warms my heart.

I knock the stick into drive and a few minutes later, we park up behind the beach.

With one hand, Jess clings on to the bag containing her cinnamon swirls for dear life, while in the other, she guards her caffeine hit. I grab my takeout cup from her and throw the beach bag I packed over my shoulder.

We head through the harsh dune grass and past the uneven and lopsided fence posts that mark a path down to the beach.

In the middle of the sand, I turn my head left and right. We are the only people out here. The sun is creeping above the water level and starting to cast a soft orange glow up the sky. Jess takes it in, staring at the sun.

I stare at her. It couldn't be more perfect.

I know I'm supposed to hold back, that I can't come on too hard and risk scaring her more than she already is. But my body steps closer to her, my chest almost touching her back.

'You really do know me, don't you?' Her words are quiet, almost lost in the sound of the ocean as she speaks, facing the sun.

I wrap my arms around her waist and rest my chin on her shoulder. I'm not sure what the right words are so I don't offer any. I just let her know I'm there, that I'll hold her if that's what she wants. I'll give her whatever she needs if she just doesn't run.

She leans her head to the side, pressing our temples together.

'When I was younger and Ruth and John first took me away, I used to wake early and head out on my own to watch the sunrise. You know the amazing thing about the sun is that, no matter where you are, no matter how insignificant or alone you feel, it's always there. Even if sometimes it's hiding behind a cloud. It's always there. And it's everyone's sun. No matter if you're on the Earth or just... somewhere, you're looking at the same sun as everyone else. There were days I missed my parents so much, I would stare at the sun as it rose, knowing that they were looking at it too, wherever they were.'

'They'll be looking at it now,' I tell her.

She closes her eyes and seems to sink into my hold a little more. 'I used to wake up feeling... dark and cold. I'd have had a bad dream or I'd have gone to sleep with bad thoughts. And when I watched the sunrise, I would steal the heat from the sun and make it warm my dark thoughts. And I would tell myself, it's a new day. You can try again. Maybe today will be easier. Maybe today good things will happen.'

She stirs in my arms until I release her. I wonder what she's doing until I see her put her coffee cup down in the sand, then she takes mine from me and places it next to hers. Then, from nowhere, she clenches her fists around the chest of my hoody and pulls me to her, lifting my cap and crashing her lips against mine.

It's a surprise. It's the best surprise I could have hoped for this morning. She doesn't open her mouth; she just lets her lips linger against mine. And I let her. I stroke my hands through her hair and enjoy the soft flesh of her lips. I let her pour everything she feels, everything that hurts her, everything she loves, and everything she fears, into me. I take it from her and I hold her to me.

When we separate, she looks down to her feet. But I want to see those eyes. I want to see the things she won't voice. I tuck my knuckle under her chin and encourage her to look at me.

She is afraid. She's terrified. And I hate that she is. But I also feel hope. If she's afraid, she might be feeling just a fraction of the emotion that's knocking me sideways.

'Don't be afraid, Jess. Don't be afraid.'

'I can't change the habits of a lifetime, Jake.' She bites her lip and her eyes cloud.

'Then let go. Don't think. Let me be with you today. Can you do that for me? Can we just be us, just be together?' Her lips slowly curve up and she nods. I wink at her. 'Atta girl.'

She laughs and thumps me in the chest. 'Keep patronizing me and you'll have to sleep with one eye open.'

'Quaking, Jess. Seriously, I'm quaking.'

Rolling her eyes playfully, she sits down on the sand. 'You'll be sorry when I don't give you one of these cinnamon swirls.'

I plant myself down on the sand next to her, both of us facing the sun, our knees pulled up. 'That's not funny. It's a step too far. You always go too far, don't you?'

She rocks into my side, smiling as she holds the open brown bag. We watch the sun's rays burst into a fan of bright beams as we drink coffee and eat sweet bread. Something tells me that somehow, at some point, we'll be fine.

Once the sun is up, I stand, pulling off my hoody and T-shirt so I'm just in my board shorts. 'You coming?'

Jess swivels to look at me, and oh yeah, she looks. 'In the sea? Won't it be cold?'

'I'll warm you up. Plus, you're going to have to get used to it for what I've got planned later.'

She rises to her feet. 'What have you got planned?'

I shrug. 'A surprise. And, by the way, you totally just checked me out.'

She gasps. 'I did not!'

'Oh yeah, babe, you did. Hey, I'm not hating. That's why I go to the gym – enjoy it. I'm only pointing out that I get a free ogle when you strip down to that itsy-bitsy bikini.'

She drops her head back with a guffaw but she does take her sweater over her head and slips her shorts down her thighs. And I watch. Oh yes, I do.

'Come on!' I jog down to the ocean's edge and she follows but stops short of the water.

'It's cold!' She starts running back to our plot in the sand but I scoop an arm around her waist and lift her, her back to my chest, her legs flailing, her lungs screaming at full capacity, and I throw myself under the water, bringing her with me.

We come up, fighting to catch our breath.

'Fuck, it is cold!' I shout, a little too high-pitched.

'Oh, what happened to Mister Macho?' she asks, and begins to imitate me. '*Babe, I go to the gym so you can stare at my pecs. Babe, I'm so hot, all women want me and men want to be me.*'

'You know what you get for that?'

I lift her over my shoulder and dunk us under the water again. We're deeper this time and she can't touch the bottom when we surface, so I lift her around my waist and hold her up.

'It doesn't get any fucking warmer.'

She shivers as she shakes her head but she makes no move to get out of the water. She drops her head to my shoulder and I hold her, slowly turning us in the water, rocking up and down with the waves. I don't know how long we stay that way but the cold of the water stops affecting me and I feel warmer than I have in three years.

Eventually, I ask, 'Have you fallen asleep, there?'

Her words vibrate against my neck. 'You couldn't blame me since you dragged me out in the middle of the night.'

'Oh, I thought you were going to say you were exhausted from our wild night of passion.'

I feel her laughter reverberate through my body.

'We need to check on the time. I told you we have plans.'

She sits back straighter, leaning away from my chest to look at me, and I rub the wet hair that's pressed to her temple behind her ear. 'What are we doing?'

'You'll see.' I walk us out of the water and set her down in the sand. It's six fifty-five – excellent planning.

'Don't we need to pack up?' she asks as I walk past our towels and bag, only stopping to grab my wallet.

'Nope.'

Giggling, she runs to catch up to me. 'You're still not going to tell me, are you?'

I wrap an arm around her shoulders. 'Nope.'

She leans harder into my side. Damn, I love when this girl is happy.

'Here we are.' I nod to the surf shack in front of us and take my arm from her shoulder. 'How do you feel about taking a surf lesson with me?'

She tilts her head to one side, a glint in her eye, a smirk on her lips. 'Surfing?'

'I thought it would be cool to try something new together.'

'And you chose surfing?'

I nod, wondering whether I called this massively wrong. She's usually up for fun stuff.

'Jake?' A guy about my age walks out of the shack, his hand out for me to shake, the wet suit that hangs down around his waist, leaving his chest exposed, a dead giveaway as to who I'm taking to. That and his mass of wavy, blond hair.

I take his hand. 'Heath?'

'The very man. You must be Jess.' He shakes her hand too and doesn't even check her out, despite the fact she looks crazy hot in her bold print bikini. 'Have either of you guys surfed before?'

I tell him no. 'But I pick up all sports fairly quickly. Spend as much time with Jess as you need.'

She tuts and her eyes widen as she scoffs the way she does when she thinks I'm being a dick.

'Sorry, babe, but surfing is tough. I want you to be safe.'

'No, thanks, I appreciate it. Like you say, you're so good at all sports. I mean, you hardly need a lesson.'

'Do I need to let you two have a domestic?' Heath asks.

'No, we're good,' Jess tells him.

'All right then, let's get you fixed up with some wet suits and boards and we'll go through the basics.'

Once the three of us are zipped in, we carry our boards onto the beach and set them down on the hard sand by the water.

'We're going to practice popping up onto the board,' Heath tells us. He demonstrates, moving from lying on the board to planting his hands on the sides and popping up to stand in the middle. Jess and I give it a go. After a few rounds of popping, I'm wondering whether Jess will be able to cope with this in the water. It's tougher than I thought.

'Ready to catch some waves?' Heath asks, standing and bringing his board under his arm.

'I'm ready. Jess, are you still up for it?'

She looks at the water, then at her board. 'I'll try. I can always stop if it's too difficult, right?'

'Sure you can, babe. We'll stop whenever you want.'

We fasten our ankle straps and follow Heath into the water. He shows us how to paddle out and the three of us set off. I get a buzz of excitement as I see the mounting waves. But I also worry about Jess in the rough water.

When we get out beyond the closest wave breaks, we sit on our boards and Heath talks us through catching the wave. 'If you don't feel confident, you can start on your knees,' he says.

We wait for minutes in the water and my adrenalin builds.

'We're going to catch this one, guys,' Heath says. 'We're just going to practice popping and getting our balance this time. Get a feel for being up on the board.'

The wave comes and we paddle until Heath calls, 'Now!'

We all make it up on the boards, with Heath staying upright but Jess and I falling off to the side. We paddle back out to the same spot and wait again. Jess reties her hair and wipes her nose as she watches the rolling water.

'Are you okay?' I ask her.

She nods but doesn't speak. She seems nervous.

'Okay, guys, this is a big one. Are you up for it?'

'I'm in,' I say, looking at Jess.

She nods tightly. 'Yeah. I'm in.'

'All right then. Let's do it.'

The wave builds and, crap, it's bigger than the last one. I'm about to tell Jess not to go but she starts paddling forward.

Looks like I'm going.

I paddle faster and faster. When the wave comes, I pop up but, mother, it's huge and fast. I manage to stand for a split second before being pushed under the water. I kick up hard, fighting the drag of the undertow, desperate to find Jess.

When I break the surface, I look around me, and finally see her, riding the wave like a pro, fisting the air and laughing before she dives off the board and under the water.

'Looks like you brought a hustler,' Heath says, paddling back toward me, laughing hard. 'She's definitely done that before, dude.'

'She freaking played me.'

Jess comes paddling out to us and shrugs when she comes up to sit on her board next to me.

'You can surf?' I ask.

'I traveled the world for fifteen years, Jake. Yes, I surf.' She drops her voice, imitating me. '*But, babe, are you sure you'll be okay? It's just I'm so great, I pick up everything real easily. I'm such a maaaan.*'

I kick up water and she splashes me back as all three of enjoy her wit.

After my surf lesson and Jess's refresher, we grab some fries and take them down to our towels on the beach.

'Where did you learn to surf?' I ask her, dunking one of my fries in her ketchup because mine is gone.

'Manly Beach in Australia. I surfed a few hotspots as I traveled around. I haven't been out on the water since I moved back to the UK, though.'

'You know what I love?'

'That I have tomato ketchup left for you to steal, which you need to stop doing, by the way, before I stab you with my fork.'

I snort-laugh. 'Besides that. I love that you can still surprise me. I can finish your sentences. I can predict what you're going to say before you say it. I can tell how you're feeling from the shade of your irises. I know what you're thinking every time you roll your eyes. But I love that there's still so much to find out about you, Jess.'

Her eyes lock on mine for silent seconds. Then she looks down as if her fries are the most interesting thing in the world. But I see the lift of her cheeks and know she's smiling.

I ball my food packaging up and stuff it into the waste bag that's pinned down by a bottle of water. When she still hasn't looked at me, I lean forward, steal a fry and make a point of taking more ketchup on that fry than I should have had on ten.

It gets her attention, even though her jaw drops as she looks at me. I go to put the potato in my mouth. Before it gets home, Jess dives on me, knocking me back in the sand and taking the food in her mouth, nipping my fingers in her teeth as she does.

She shoves my arms above my head and I let her think she's got me as she pins them to the sand. I like the way she's straddling me in her bikini.

'You know what else would surprise me?' I say.

She shakes her head.

'If you were to slip out of those little panties and ride me on this beach.'

Her eyes widen. 'You, sir, are a pervert.'

'I thought you were a wild one, huh? Where did exciting Jess go?'

'She went to jail. For having sex on a beach surrounded by people.'

My laughter is caught by her mouth crashing against mine. I wrap my arms around her and hold her to me as I part her lips with my tongue, not wanting to tell her, panties still on, she surprised me anyway, because this kiss is too damn good to stop.

I roll us on the towels so she's on her back, her legs wrapped around my waist. She strokes her hand through my hair and gazes into my eyes.

Is she with me? Is she feeling what I'm feeling?

God, I hope so, because right now, it's taking all the strength I have not to tell her I'm so in love with her, it hurts.

* * *

Walking back to the beach with four bottles of beer, I watch Jess, sitting on her towel, now back in her hoody and shorts, her knees tucked into her chest as the day's light dwindles. As simple as it's been, today has been one of the best of my life and I can't help wondering what's happening in that mind of hers. I'm hoping she's feeling some of what is filling my entire body with warmth.

I slide to the ground behind her, positioning my legs either side, and I hold out the opened bottles. She digs two into the sand and keeps one for herself.

'You smell fresh,' I tell her, inhaling the scent of outdoors from her hair.

She leans against me and presses her lips to my arm through my sweater. 'You smell of you,' she says quietly.

If we could never move, if we could stay in this moment forever, I would.

We drink our first beers in silence, holding on to each other. It's a kind of peace I've never felt before, and never known I would love.

As Jess switches our empty bottles for full ones, I finally ask what I'm dying to know. 'What are you thinking?'

'Not much.' She chuckles in my hold and I nudge into her neck, biting her earlobe in response to her sarcasm. That's the Brit in her. They love their sarcasm.

'You never mentioned Emily being at the house when you got back from fishing.'

Well, that wasn't exactly what I was expecting her to come out with but I'm sure at some point, probably when I can't sleep at three in the morning, I'll make the connection to what she's actually thinking in that busy head of hers.

'I hardly realized she was there, to be honest. In case you didn't notice, I had eyes for only one woman at that moment.'

She bites my arm. 'Was it strange for you, that she was there?'

'No. I'm used to Emily being around more than her not being around. What was she doing there, though?'

'I invited her.'

I tighten my hold on her as she shivers. 'I have no issue with that, but can I ask why?'

'Because I wanted to get to know her better. I figure she's back in your life now and I'd like it if we could be friends.'

'When you say that, I hope you understand that if she's back in my life, she's there as a friend. You know that, right?'

She takes a swig from her bottle instead of answering my question. I take the bottle from her mouth and shift so I'm looking her in the eye.

'Hey. You know that, right? I don't want her to be any more than that. Until very recently, I didn't appreciate that. I didn't...'

My words come and go, getting lost between my head and my tongue.

Jess sets her bottle in the sand and twists to face me, coming up to her knees and taking my cheeks in her hands. 'It's okay, Jake. You don't have to have all the answers. You've only just started talking to each other again. I only want you to know that... I like her. And she loves you. I adore her for that.'

I growl and sit forward, forcing her to lie back in the sand. 'I adore you, Jess.'

She bites her lip and raises a brow as I come to hover above her. 'I hope we're clear on what my feelings are for Emily,' she says, "cause I don't adore her like I want to roll around naked in the sand with her.'

I bend, brushing my lips gently across her neck until goosebumps form on her skin. 'That's a shame. I think I could be into you rolling around naked with women.'

She laughs so hard, her chest rocks against mine. She slaps a hand across my back and lifts her head, reaching up and putting her hands on my nape. I waste no time in kissing her.

We roll in the sand, me on top, her on top, our lips never parting and I wonder how, in two years, we have managed to live without making out like this. I feel like a teenager, not only because we're kissing and grinding on a beach, but because there's a childish excitement coursing through my body, like a kid starting something new and exhilarating. I'm on the fastest rollercoaster known to man and I'm not afraid of the twists and turns to come. I'm not afraid of dangling upside down with my feet in the air. I want it all. I want the ride, however it comes. I want Jess.

The sky is black by the time a beagle pushes its nose between Jess's face and mine. 'What the fu—?'

'Oh my gosh, I'm so sorry.'

Jess and I lift our heads to a woman who looks like she's running through syrup as her feet dig in the sand, coming to retrieve her dog. I wink at Jess, finally breaking away from her. I stand and take hold of...

'Roger, I've told you, people don't want to play.'

I keep hold of the dog's collar until the owner reaches us. Jess adjusts her sweater where my hands may, or may not, have been creeping up. Hey, it's dark.

'Your dog is called Roger?' I ask.

The woman clips him on to a leash. 'He's jolly. Like Jolly Roger.'

I smile, partly because that's amusing, mostly because I feel high on life.

'Cute,' I say.

When she's gone, Jess and I pack up our things. Reluctantly, I lead her back to the truck and close the passenger door behind her as she slips inside. Not before giving her one last kiss.

She connects her cell to Brooks' car port and leans back in her seat, her bare feet up on the dash, the wind blowing her hair, her lips swollen and inviting. She takes hold of my hand and her cheeks lift as she stares out at the clear night sky.

My expression matches hers as I pull into the open road because, for the first time today, I'm thinking she might beat her fears and stay.

17

JAKE

'You don't have to start opening doors for me and minding your p's and q's because you dry-humped me sober, you know.'

I shake my head as I offer my hand to Jess and help her out of the truck. I step into her, nudging her back against the truck. 'Always so, so classy.'

Just as I move in for a heated kiss, Brooks comes out of the house. 'I thought I heard the truck. Have you had a good day?'

Jess clears her throat and looks at the ground as the street light illuminates the red rising on her cheeks and neck. Her awkwardness amuses me.

'We've had a good day,' I respond. 'Are you coming to make sure I haven't beaten up the truck?'

'In part. The main reason I'm out here is to forewarn you that Emily is here.'

I shrug and glance at Jess. 'That's cool, right?'

'Of course, yes.'

'It's Ems, Brooks. We're good now. We've talked.'

One side of his face twists and he scratches the thick stubble around his jaw. 'Right. Thing is, she's not alone.'

My body stiffens without it even receiving the warning messages from my brain. It can't receive messages from my brain because my brain has gone into code freaking red.

'She brought him?'

'Yeah. Listen, buddy, I came to tell you because I'm willing to bet you want to do to that guy what I'd want to do to him.'

My breaths come in heavy, long drags. The guy who acted like my friend, who I trusted with my secrets, and then fucking betrayed me. The way I was brought up, family and friends are everything. They aren't something you screw over for no good reason. My fists clench at my sides.

'You came out here to stop me.'

Brooks holds up a hand, as if in surrender. 'No. I came to forewarn you so you can choose what you're putting into play, offense or defense.'

'Defense? There's no defense for the shit he pulled.'

I think Jess says something in the background but I'm already lost to rage. The rage I've let simmer for three years. Rage so strong, I forget I'm walking through my brother's house, that my friends are sitting around by the pool having pleasant evening drinks. I step out to the deck and watch the bastard, grinning and joking with my friends, my family. He doesn't deserve to be around these people.

Emily clocks me first and stands as I make my way to the group. She plants a hand on my chest. I'm het up enough to knock someone out of the way, so it's a dangerous move, but I control myself.

'Take it easy, Jake,' she says, glaring into my eyes.

'Emily, step aside.'

Brandon stands and I see Drew rise in my peripheral vision.

'Emily,' he warns, 'this is between them.'

She stays between us, her hand still on my chest. I call out to Brandon across her shoulder. 'What the fuck are you doing here? You have no goddamn right to be here.'

'Relax, bro. What's done is done. It's in the p—'

'Oh hell, you did not call me your bro.'

Wisely, Emily steps aside as I launch myself at the man I once considered a good guy.

'Brandon! Jake!'

I collide with Brandon and we tumble back onto the pathway leading down to the beach. I shove him off me, and he lands yards further down the sand than I do. He staggers to his feet, his white shirt coming untucked from his chinos. Pretentious wanker. Who sits around the beach in chinos and a fucking shirt?

'You busted my lip,' he whines.

'I'm gonna bust a lot more than your lip.'

I charge back at him, knocking him to the ground again. I drive my fist into his jaw, knocking his head to the side. I raise my fist again but before it lands, searing pain burns from my crotch and brings vomit to my throat. I roll to the side, covering my dick and balls, in agony from Brandon's knee.

'That's a low blow,' I snarl.

He dives on top of me and moves to drive an elbow in my face. Same old moves I've seen him use in drunken fights a thousand times. I block his elbow and crash a fist into his ribs.

'Brandon!' The voice is Emily's but I see the others running onto the beach.

'Take her up there,' I hear Brooks say. 'Let's leave them to it.'

I smash another blow into Brandon's side and he falls off me, gasping for breath.

'You two gonna kill each other?' Drew asks.

I glance at Brandon, who is curled into a ball, blood running from his nose and onto his pompous shirt as he squirms. I can't stand the guy but I'm not about to beat someone to death either. I shake my head at Drew and Brooks, who are standing side by side, their arms folded across their chests.

They head back up to the house as I come up to sit and face out to sea, my arms draped loosely over my knees, rubbing my right knuckles with my left hand. Brandon coughs and splutters as he crawls up to sit next to me, mirroring my position.

'Feel better for that, asshole?'

'It's something I should have done three years ago, fucking traitor.'

'Traitor? Jake, I hated myself for it. I hated listening to you spill your guts about Ems then...'

'Then going back to our house and screwing her?'

He drags in a breath so deep, it makes him cough. 'Yeah, actually. Yeah. I felt fucking horrible. I still do. I wasn't going to come tonight but Ems said you guys were patching things up and, damn it, man, I wanted to be able to do the same.'

'We can never be friends again, Brandon. Not after what you did.'

'Jake, you didn't love her. Not like that. I listened to everything you said and I know how much you care about her. But you were never in love with her the way I am. You were afraid of losing her.'

I want to argue but he's right. I know that now. 'It wasn't about whether I did or didn't love her, Brandon. Fact was, I told you I did. There's such a thing as guy code.'

'I know. I messed up big time. I'm not denying it. I should have told you how I felt before making a play. Hell, maybe I should never have made a play.'

'Yeah, you got that right.'

'But I love her, Jake. I do. I did then and... fuck it.'

I take my eyes from the dark horizon and look at him. He rubs a finger under his nose and winces.

'Fuck what?' I ask, my conviction waning.

'I'm going to ask her to marry me. I want to spend my life with her.'

'Marry her? Marry my Ems?'

He pulls back from me, as if I might hit him again. Christ, he truly does love her. More than I could have, at least that way.

'It really wasn't just a lay, huh?'

'If it had been, I'm pretty certain I could have stopped myself.'

I rub a hand roughly over my jaw. 'Like hell you would have. At college, your dick was bigger than your brain. Probably still is.'

'Screw you. I've got a decent job in the city. Granted, it doesn't pay like Billy-Big-Shot's job beside me but I do well.' He looks up toward the house. I don't follow his gaze. 'I'll take care of her, Jake.'

'You'd better, Brandon. I swear to God, you hurt her, I will break you. I will end you. I'd do anything for her.'

His lips curve into a small smile. 'That's why I want you to be in our lives, Jake.'

I glance at his hand on my shoulder, then at his face. 'Christ, you going to try to kiss me next?'

He scoffs and we fall into silence. I've got to admit, it feels nice to have gotten Emily, to have gotten Brandon, out of my system. Maybe one day, probably no time soon, we can find a way to all be friends again.

As we sit watching the ebb and flow of the water, I realize, for me, there's nothing between me and the girl I want any more. Nothing except her own demons. And I hope we can get past them, because damn it, I want to be the guy holding the ring someday.

'What the hell is it with everyone proposing this week?' I mutter.

'By all accounts, you've looked pretty cozy with the brunette. Is she new?'

I raise one brow as I turn to face him. 'Keep your hands to yourself.'

He chuckles and I share the moment. For now, it feels nice.

We talk about the last few years, nothing too personal, but filling in the blanks that mutual friends haven't done for us. We talk until the lights go out at the house and Emily comes down to the beach.

'Are my boys getting along?' She slips down to the sand, nudging Brandon and me farther apart with her hips.

I drop an arm around her shoulder. 'Who died and made you chief, huh?'

'Well, when the rest of the squad is regressing, someone has to step up to the plate, right?'

'Even regressed, I'm still chief, Ems.'

She beats her chest and growls like a silverback. I laugh, fully appreciating how ridiculous Brandon and I must have looked to the others, fighting like kids in the sand.

We talk for a while but there's something missing. Someone. And I want her here. I want her by my side.

For the rest of my life.

'All right, guys. I'm out. Sleep well.'

Emily stands and kisses my cheek. I pull her into a hug, trying to tell her in that move that I'll always be there for her. 'When he screws up...'

She hits my chest but smiles, then backs into Brandon and takes hold of his hand. In some other time and place, I might have thought it was pretty cool that my best friends hooked up and fell in love.

I'm still not quite there yet.

Brandon holds out a hand and I stare at it a beat too long before I take it. 'You might need to get that nose seen to,' I tell him.

'Nah, you hit like a pussy, always have.'

'Yeah, tell me that when you've had a nose job tomorrow.'

As I head up the path to the house, making my strides larger and faster until I'm jogging, my excitement builds. I want to go to bed with my girl, even if I only get to hold her. I feel... free, somehow. It's hard to describe. It's as if socking Brandon in the face and seeing Ems, seeing them happy and still together, has given me a blank slate. I can love Jess. I *do* love Jess. I think maybe I have from the day she walked into my apartment, startled that Alex opened the door naked. From the moment we realized we both secretly like black-and-white movies. Since the first time she told me how she lost her parents and I wanted to be her protector and take care of her the way she should have been taken care of all her life.

I can hear voices coming from the bedrooms but the lights in the house are out. I climb the stairs, the glass ceilings giving me enough to see by. There's no light coming from under the bedroom door but I know she won't be sleeping yet. Jess is a night owl.

I turn on the light and instantly dim it in case she is sleeping. But the bed is empty.

'Jess?'

I walk through to the en suite but that is empty too. Her toothbrush is gone.

I open the wardrobe in the bedroom. Her clothes are gone. 'What the fuck?'

And I know.

My gut falls like I'm free-falling from a clifftop toward a bed of rocks.

She ran.

I dart from the bedroom and downstairs, running out the front door. As I reach the end of the drive, I see the taillights of a yellow cab driving away, and I know who is sitting in the back.

The night seems to grow darker and a tightness settles into my chest, making it hard to breathe, making my eyes sting.

She ran.

I stand in the middle of the road, staring in the direction of the cab, praying for it to turn around and bring her back. Knowing that won't happen.

18

JESS

People assume that when you fall in a love with a friend, it happens gradually. That it creeps up on you without a defining moment. People assume that a love that comes from the foundation of a friendship doesn't have a moment of fireworks: bangs that shock you to the core, bursts of bright color, a sense of overwhelming beauty. That your friendship simply becomes something you depend on so much that you can't let it go. You recognize everything about your friend that is truly magnificent. Sometimes, you see things others will never be blessed to see because you, and only you, know that person so well. That may be true for lots of couples who started out as friends.

But that isn't what happened with Jake and me. I knew from the moment I signed that lease to share the apartment with him and Alex there was a danger I could fall for him. I knew from the fact he quickly became the person I wanted to spend every spare second with, that I adored him, all of him.

But I can point to one moment and say, definitively, that is when I fell in love with Jake Harrington.

It was a Friday night, six months ago...

'Jess? Babes?' Jake called as I heard the door to the apartment close behind him. 'I got held up at work.'

His voice grew louder as his footsteps moved along the hallway to my bedroom.

He knocked on the door but entered anyway. He'd caught me in my underwear enough times for him to have decided he might as well invade my space whenever he felt like it. At least, that's what I used to tell him.

In reality, I never felt like Jake was intruding in my space.

'Whoa! Why are you in bed, babe?'

I blew my sore nose as a demonstration of why I was wrapped in my duvet at 7 p.m. on a Friday night, instead of getting dressed to go out.

'I've been wiped out by woman flu,' I said. The words came out more like, 'Ibe een iped out by uman blew.'

He came to sit on the edge of the bed, dipping the double mattress toward him. 'You have uman blew?'

Despite the razor blades slicing my throat, the throbbing of my head at the base of my skull, my aching muscles and my stinging nose, I laughed.

He leaned across my legs, his white shirt pulled tight over his toned hips, showing me that little bit where his muscles cut in. 'But I need my tequila partner,' he said.

'I'm sorry, you're going to have to take one for the team tonight. How about I promise to clean away my snot rags and tomorrow, when you're hungover from drinking tequila for both of us, we can suffer together watching mindless movies? I'll even succumb to those American humor ones that aren't funny at all.'

'*Ted*?'

I chuckled. 'Yes, we can watch *Ted*.'

He took me by surprise, reaching up to stroke my cheek. 'You have a temperature. Maybe you should take a few layers off? Is that my hoody?'

I looked down at the oversized, black sweatshirt. 'Oh, yeah. I needed something cozy.'

Something about that made him pause. He kept his hand on my cheek and his eyes seemed to fill with warmth. His mouth curved at one side. The smile I loved on him. It was distinctly Jake. I loved all things distinctly Jake.

'I don't want to go out without you.'

'Stop being a baby. You'll find some tart in a mini skirt, probably leather, to drink tequila with. And I'll be so wiped out on Night Nurse capsules I won't even hear you making her squeak and squeal her way through sex.'

He gave a short laugh but not the kind he would usually give me for a crude comment.

'You're the only woman I drink tequila with. If you aren't there, the tequila team isn't turning up.'

'Then you'll have to drink beer with Alex and belch all night.'

His laughter was short again and the genuine look of disappointment on his face made me feel even worse than I already felt. 'Maybe I can try.'

I wiggled my legs free from under him and pulled back the covers. I sat upright, placed my feet on the floor, and stood. As I did, yellow, purple, green and blue spots moved into my vision.

'Whoa, whoa. Jess.' I felt Jake's arms wrap around me. He caught me and brought me back down to the bed. 'Have you eaten today?'

I shook my head as he laid me down and brought the covers back over me, tucking them up to my chin.

He stroked my hair, which must have felt awful against my clammy temples, and he pressed his lips to my forehead.

'The Tequila Queen has temporarily vacated her throne,' he whispered.

My lips curved up before I closed my eyes. I could still feel his weight on the bed and the gentle touch of his fingers as I drifted into darkness.

I woke a couple of hours later. In the light of the bedside lamp, I could see I was alone. But my used tissues had been cleared away and Jake's laptop was on the bed next to me, paused on a scene I recognized from the movie *Hacksaw Ridge*.

I dragged myself up to sit, still feeling weak and drained but a little better than before my nap. As if by magic, the bedroom door opened slowly and Jake stood in the doorway, holding a tray.

'You were stirring. I figured you would be awake soon.'

'Why aren't you out?'

He didn't answer, just moved toward me and placed the tray down on the bed. 'Broccoli and stilton soup. The bread is still warm if you can manage it. Orange juice for that essential vitamin C, and water, because apparently woman flu can be severely dehydrating.'

I wanted to smile at his kindness. I wanted to thank him. But the lump in my throat that had nothing to do with my sickness wouldn't let me speak.

'You stayed in on a Friday night to make me soup?'

He moved around the bed and sat down where I assumed he'd been sitting while I slept. He hit play on *Hacksaw Ridge* and shuffled the laptop to a position where we could both watch it.

'I hope you like the soup. My mom had to talk me through making it on Skype.'

The lump was so big, it was almost choking me. 'You called your mum? You went out and bought ingredients?'

'Oh shit, babes. Why are you crying? Are you hurting? What can I do?'

It was right then. That was the moment I fell in love with Jake Harrington.

I fell in love with him as he held me to him. As I cried because he'd made me soup. As I cried because he was the first person who had ever truly wanted to take care of me since I was a girl. As I let him hold me the way my mum used to hold me when I was sick.

'My throat hurts really bad,' I sobbed.

He kissed my scalp until I pulled myself together. I ate my soup and we watched what was left of the film. The whole time, my heartbeat grew stronger and faster.

No. No, Jess. You cannot be in love with Jake. He means too much. He's too good. You can't love him because it will be the end of you both.

19

JAKE

A hand on my shoulder wakes me. I lift my head from the breakfast counter and immediately look at the phone in my hand. She hasn't returned any of my calls. She hasn't replied to my text messages asking where the hell she is and why she ran out without speaking to me. Nothing.

'Brooks and Drew are dragging my ass for a run,' Kit said. 'You want to come and clear your head?'

I flex the knuckles of my right hand and wince. Kit could be asking if I want to clear my head after punching Brandon last night. But the fact he doesn't ask why I was sleeping at the breakfast counter in the clothes I was wearing last night tells me he knows Jess has gone.

Maybe he knew she packed up her things. Maybe he saw her leave in a cab. Or maybe he heard me shouting her name in the middle of the street as her cab drove away.

Being with Jess yesterday was everything. What cuts me more than the fact she ran is that I think I'd take the churning in my gut right now a thousand times again to have had yesterday just once more.

I massage my right knuckles with my left hand and bring my hands to my chin as I replay every perfect moment. My mind gets to walking onto the deck last night when I ruined everything.

She thinks I fought for Emily. Even though I told her I'm not into her like that, I'm not an idiot, I can see how it must have looked.

Jess's default mindset is to find every reason not to fall in love. And fuck if I didn't give her the biggest reason to hate me.

I spent a day showing her in every way how much I wanted her. Doing everything short of saying the three words I feel with every beat of my heart. She would have been scared enough. Then I acted like a jackass and really blew it.

'Jake?'

I dart my head to Kit. 'Ah, yeah, give me five.'

Upstairs, I change into my sweats and check my cell one last time. Still nothing.

All I know is, she can't have gone far because our flight is Sunday. I'd bank on her still taking that same flight home.

I fire another message:

Jess, please. Stop running. Talk to me. I'm sorry.

I meet Brooks, Drew and Kit on the driveway.

'Do you want to talk about it?' Drew asks.

I crack my neck and bend my foot up to my butt to stretch my quads. 'How about you guys make me run until I'm only thinking about my next breath?'

'Hell, yeah, I can do that,' Brooks says. 'Let's go, Jakey.'

For the first four clicks, all I think about is Jess. About yesterday. About every amazing day since I've met her. Wondering whether she's in love with me.

If she didn't feel something, she wouldn't have cared whether I fought over Emily, would she?

I thank the running gods when Brooks picks up his pace and we drive forward, pounding the streets harder, until my ability to think clearly is gone.

You can always rely on Brooks to take you out of your head when you need him.

We finish the run along the beach, the sand putting the final nail in the coffin for our dead thighs. Kit keeps up relatively well, either because he's getting in shape, or because a week of indulgent food and booze mean Brooks, Drew and I are slower than usual, though he's still breathing like he smoked sixty cigars this morning. Brooks, Drew and I are breathing hard too, and I'm sweating from places I never knew I could sweat from.

Cold water and all, we take off our sneakers and caps and throw ourselves into the ocean.

I dunk my head under the water and flick my wet hair from my eyes after I surface.

'So, are we going to talk about why Jess left last night?' Kit asks. 'Am I the only one who can see the huge, enormous, fat elephant in the room?'

'Ah, that was ripe for a fat Kit joke,' Brooks says, rubbing his hands over his face. 'It's a shame we got you thin.'

For the first time this morning, something amuses me.

'It seems pretty obvious why she left. I crossed the line with her, made us something more than we agreed we would be, then she assumed I struck out at Brandon because I'm still into Emily. She thinks I played her and it fucking kills me.'

'Is she right?' Drew asks.

'She couldn't be more wrong. I just needed to... Brandon and I had unfinished business, that's all last night was. And, by the way, I'm sorry for messing up your night like that. I'll apologize to the girls when they're up.'

'Hey, don't worry about it. People pay good money to watch fights like that and we had free ringside seats,' Kit says, making me chuckle.

'Yeah, well, it's not exactly what you want on a night away with your friends, so I am sorry.' Then a thought occurs to me. 'Shit, Drew, last night wasn't the big night, was it?'

'Big night?' Kit asks as Drew raises a brow at me.

'Aaaand that's the real fat elephant in the room. Sorry two times, bro.' Drew smashes water at me.

'Oh, is this the part where you tell me the purpose of this week is for you to propose to Becky?' Kit asks.

'What the...?' Drew lifts his hands from the water as if he's raising the roof.

'Ah, come on, it's obvious. It's been in the cards since you fell for her cakes. And I mean cakes; that wasn't some kind of reference to soggy bottoms or cream centers.'

'What goes on in your head?' Drew asks. 'Yes, all right. I'm proposing to Becky this week. And, if it's not too much trouble, could you all be around and not 'cause any bloody beach fights at the party I have planned tomorrow night?'

'Party?' I ask. 'You assume she'll say yes, huh?'

I get dunked this time, Drew pushing his entire body weight on my shoulders. I wrestle my way back up and dunk him in return.

'I have a party planned on the assumption she'll say yes but that's why I haven't told you about it. It's nothing over the top; Becky would hate that. I've just got caterers coming in to make sure she can relax. And I had to forewarn Mom and Millie. Can you imagine if I didn't let Mom in on the secret and she found out I'd celebrated with you bunch of jackasses?'

I whistle. 'Ohhhh, you'd have been in hell.'

'Seriously though, Drew,' Brooks says. 'It's Friday, buddy. Time is running out.'

'I know. Tonight is the night. If slippery tongue can keep his mouth shut for a few hours, we should be all good.'

'Slippery tongue?' Kit asks. 'Is that supposed to be me? Man, name one secret I've ever shared of yours.'

'Let me see... when I had a crush on Lana Jonson in sophomore year? When I stole the cheer squad's pom-poms with the rest of the football team? When I bet you Marty would lose his first case in court? When...'

'All right, I get it. I can't hold my water. I guess you'd better get a move on in that case.' Kit winks and Brooks and I laugh, more at the fear that takes over Drew's face than Kit's words.

'Just don't put the ring in a glass of champagne or something,' I say, as we walk out of the water. 'I've heard stories of people choking and having to get the diamond flushed out of them in the ER.'

'Yeah, I wouldn't go for putting it in a cake either,' Brooks says. 'Becky would kick your ass if you ruined a good cake.'

'Plus, she might crack a tooth or something on the size of the rock I imagine you've got for her,' Kit adds.

'Thanks, guys. Like I wasn't nervous enough. I feel like I'm about to pitch my first little league game and the rest of the team is ten years older than me.'

'While I appreciate the sentiment, that makes no sense,' I tell him.

'Damn it, sometimes I wish I hadn't put you through college and given you a brain. There was a time you would hang on every word I said.'

* * *

By noon, there's still no word from Jess. I shoot her another text message as we all sit around the pool. The others are starting their first round of margaritas.

At least let me know you are safe.

Dots appear across the screen as if she's typing. Then they disappear. I sit up, straddling the lounger, hopeful. The dots come again and disappear again. All the while, I gawp at my cell. They come again, then...

I'm safe.

'I'm safe? That's it!?'

I growl and flop back on the sunbed, turning up the music in my ears to drown out the chatter of the others and pulling my cap over my face, half because I'm frustrated and hurt and so enraged with myself for being such an idiot, I could cry. Half because I want to be alone, in darkness, where I can think.

Is that what you're doing, Jess? Do you just need time to think?

Argh, thinking is dangerous! What if she doesn't want anything more than to be my friend? How could we possibly go back? God knows I would if that's what it takes for me to keep her. But can I pretend I don't have feelings for her when what I do feel is tearing me apart? What if she's thinking she'll move on, run to another city or country, or the other side of the world, like she's done so many times before? The thought is like taking a round from an AK-47 to my torso; it hurts going in, it blows me apart as it comes out.

Bright light pierces my eyelids as cap is pulled from my face and my earbuds yanked out of my ears. Sarah is wrapped in a towel and sits down on my lounger, tapping my legs to tell me to move them aside.

'I love how dramatic you boys are. Do you know that? It keeps things interesting, having to fix your love lives for you. It makes me feel like I live in a movie or something. Of course, I'd be as fabulous as Audrey Hepburn or Marilyn Monroe. Audrey is more me, I think, with the brown hair. And those gorgeous pearls.'

'I've no doubt you would be more fabulous than Audrey, Sarah, but now who's being dramatic?'

'Oh, right, ha. I do have a point I want to make.'

'By all means.'

She sips her margarita and licks the salt that has transferred from the rim of her glass to her finger.

'Here's what I think. One, you and Jess know everything about each other and still worship each other. A-ah, no talking, Jakey. This is Sarah's spotlight.' She holds up two fingers. 'Two, somewhere along the line, one or both of you decided it would be a good idea to start sleeping together. Be quiet! The fact is, you had your reasons for doing that but for sure, you were sexually attracted to each other.'

'It was her idea, initially.'

'Which only serves to prove the point I'm going to make. Keep listening.' She holds up three fingers. 'Three, if you hadn't already realized it, you have both fallen for each other. It seems to me, you both have shit to figure out because... well, who doesn't, right? Jake, silence. For your part, the mess is obvious. You were messed up over the Emily and Brandon thing. Now, it seems you worked out that you were never actually into Emily and, while I hate to say it, those two are cute together.'

'Maybe now is a good time to race to the finish line.'

She shrugs and sips her drink again, taking her time and taking control, just how Sarah likes things. 'The rest I have to guess at but let me tell you, I'm very good at reading people, and I'm very good at reading love. Oh, don't look like that; everyone around this pool can see you are 100 per cent, prime time in love with Jess.'

'You stole that line from Meg Ryan in *Top Gun*. I use it myself.'

'I did. But I added my own twist. Anyway, my guess is this. Jess is in love with you too.'

I swallow hard. 'You think so?'

'Baby, I know so. And I'm willing to bet she's a runner.'

I snort. 'What makes you think that?'

'I know about her parents and her ex-fiancé. I'm certain there's a heck of a lot more that's gone on in her life that you know and I don't. So, yes, the fact she's not here now tells me she's a runner but so does her past, Jake. Of course she'd run.'

'You think I didn't know that? I tried not to come on too hard.'

She smiles and leans her head to one side, as if she knows something I don't. 'Oh, Jake, don't you get it? This isn't about you coming on too hard.'

'Then please enlighten me as to what the hell it is about.'

'For the record, your tone is a little shitty. I don't approve.'

'Sorry.'

'Accepted. When we were at the bar the other night and you got all silverback over Brandon and Emily walking in and Jess kissed you, I spoke to her outside. She was upset, Jake. Not because she thought you wanted Emily but because she was afraid she might be jealous.'

I lift my cap and scratch my head. 'You're losing me.'

She rolls her eyes and sighs. 'You boys are so damn dumb. She was afraid, Jakey. If she was jealous that meant she wanted you to herself. Are you following now? She loves you, Jake.'

'But if... I mean... why run then?'

'You said she was the one who suggested sleeping together? Well, I could be wrong but I'm going to throw out the idea that she thought she could control how she felt about you if you could be friends and she could control how much she wanted to...you know, bang bang, hump hump.'

'Bang bang, hump hump?' I laugh. It's short-lived but an unbeliev-able feat given the way I feel today. When I stop, I think about what Sarah is saying. 'So, when I realized I wanted to be with her...'

'You took away the safety net. She was relying on you being too messed up over Emily to want more than your friends-with-benefits arrangement.'

'She knows I don't want Emily.'

'Yep.'

'She knows I want her.'

'Yep.'

'And she's running because she wants me too?'

'Ting, ting, ting! Jackpot, Jakey.'

'She is afraid. Of course she's afraid.'

'There you go.'

I jump up from the lounger. 'She fucking loves me.'

Sarah laughs. 'Well, what are you doing moping around the pool?'

My excitement dies in an instant as I look at Sarah. 'I have no idea where she is.'

She leans her head to the side again, as if I'm a dumbass. 'Your flight is Sunday. She told me she's never been to New York before. And she's a traveler. How hard is the math?'

'You think she's in the city?'

'You know her inside and out, Jake.' She steps up to me and places her hand on my chest. 'Start thinking with this. Where does your heart tell you she is?'

I wish I knew. Goddamn it, I wish I could find her and say some-thing, anything to make her give us a shot.

'I don't kn— *Home Alone.*'

'What?'

'*Home Alone.* The bird woman. The Plaza.'

'Are you having some kind of seizure right now?'

'Sarah, I fucking love you.' I grab her head and kiss her temple. 'I've got to go.'

'Ah, you boys are so crazy. I adore it. Well, go, stop staring at me. Go get your girlfriend.'

'Drew, good luck, bro! I'll be back!' I call as I run into the house and upstairs. I consider packing things into a bag but I can't wait. I need to find her. I grab my wallet and head downstairs.

'Hey! You might need these!' Brooks throws me the keys to his truck and I catch them.

Marty comes over, dangling another set of keys. 'Bullshit, mine's quicker. I'm glad you pulled your head out of your ass. And if you hurt my car, I'll hurt you right back, Jake, whether you're Drew's brother or not.'

'I knew there had to be something I like about you, Marty. Thanks, man.'

I take his keys and make for the door.

'These things never work out. I'm going to enjoy the show, that's all!' he calls after me.

'Save your cynical bachelor shit, Marty. You just haven't found the right girl,' I shout back.

Within seconds, I'm hurtling out of the driveway in the direction of the city.

20

JAKE

My buzz dies somewhere along the I-495. Not only do I not have a clue as to where Jess is, beyond a loose idea that she wanted to run like Macaulay Culkin did in *Home Alone 2*, but even if I see her, she's running scared and I have no idea what I could do or say to convince her to take a chance on us.

I make it into the city in record time. Marty's wheels are hot! I park in a garage close to The Plaza, the hotel Macaulay Culkin stays in in *Home Alone 2*, thinking that I might have lost my mind. But this is the only thing I have to go on.

I take out my cell: nothing from Jess. I send her a message:

I'm in the city. Where are you?

I wait for a reply that doesn't come, then I Google, *Macaulay Culkin Run Home Alone 2*. Yep, I've definitely lost it.

My stomach sinks when I see that half the scenes featured in the movie were actually shot in Chicago. 'Give a guy a break!'

People on the sidewalk give me peculiar looks but they don't appreciate how damn frustrated I am right now.

'Duncan's Toy Chest isn't real! Goddamn it!'

That doesn't seem to give people the answers they were looking for, just garners me more peculiar looks.

I seem to have driven into bad weather in the city. The buildings hold on to warmth but the sky is gray and threatening to rain. Oh, yeah, and I'm still in the shorts and a T-shirt I was wearing beside the pool before I lost my head and flew to the city.

I know Jess doesn't have much money, which is part of the reason I know she won't have changed her flight; I also know she'll try to keep her bargain with her dad to run like Macaulay.

The bellhop at The Plaza stares at my attire as he holds the door for me. Maybe one day, I will come back here in my suit and stay in a suite and run up a tab he can't afford. Look down your goddamn nose at me?

The receptionist is full of smiles.

'Hi, I'm looking for a... friend, Jess Walters. I think she might have booked in here last night, well, early this morning.'

'I'm terribly sorry, sir, but I can't give you information about guests. This is The Plaza.'

Correction: she is snooty!

'Look, I am begging you. I drove from the Hamptons in record time to find this girl, *the* girl, and tell her that I can't live without her, so, please, help me out here.'

'That's so sweet.'

'Thanks. So, can you help me out?'

'No. I'm sorry.'

I drag air into my nostrils, feeling them flare. Slapping a hand down on the counter, I search the faces in the atrium. I move through the bars and restaurants, receiving dirty looks for the fact I'm wearing shorts, but still don't find any sign of Jess.

I stand back out on the sidewalk as the heavens open. Looking up to the sky, watching rain drops before they land on me, I realize Jess won't be inside. She once told me, wherever we are, it's the same rain, the same wind, the same sun. Weather connects us. She'll be out here, under the rain, feeling closer to her dad than ever.

That thought makes something else occur to me. I may not be able to work out Macaulay's running route but I do know that the bird woman lived in Central Park.

I enter the park, my head down to stop rain hitting my eyes, and head in the direction of Gapstow Bridge over the pond, passing two tourists in yellow duck ponchos. Cute, if you're into that kind of thing, I suppose.

Thanks to the rain, the bridge is empty. For the record, there's no Pigeon Lady here. Nor is Kevin McCallister. It's just me, in the pouring rain, leaning my forearms on the bridge and watching ripples in the pond from the raindrops.

I check my cell again. Nothing. A group of teenagers comes by, talking excitedly about a movie they've seen.

Forty minutes have passed and still nothing.

The rain stops but the sky stays gray. I shiver under the cold of my sodden clothes.

My cell now tells me I've been here for an hour and a half.

I start thinking of my next steps but I come up empty. The reality is, Jess may have been here already. She may never come. She may come tomorrow.

A man stops with a woman I take to be his wife. They ask for directions and I point them toward Hell's Kitchen.

I lean back against the bridge and look at the buildings towering over the park. I take in the lush green, knowing it will soon turn to the brightest orange for fall.

God, I love New York.

The rain comes again, spitting at first, then bouncing around my bare shins. Fantastic.

Closing my eyes, I raise my head to the sky and let the weather cover my face, asking the sky, or the people up there, to help me out here.

'You found me.'

Her voice fills my ears, my chest, and warms my chilled bones. I open my eyes and see she really is there, standing in front of me, her hair wet, the collar of her leather jacket pulled up, her jeans soaked through. She couldn't look more mesmerizing.

She moves closer to me and I turn from the water to face her.

'I knew you wouldn't leave the city without coming here.'

'I could have already been. I could have come tomorrow. What were you going to do, sleep out here?'

Her eyes are full, her brown irises bold yet fearful.

'If that's what it took, yes.'

She holds her next blink for seconds. 'You're certifiably nuts.'

I take the opportunity to step closer to her, so close I can almost feel her heart pounding in her chest. Close enough I can smell her, the way her perfume blends with something that's just her. The smell of home.

'If I'm crazy, Jess, it's over you.'

She opens her eyes and looks into mine. 'What are you doing here?'

'I came to set you straight on a few things.'

'Is that right?'

'That's right. First, I have no feelings for Emily beyond the platonic.'

She nods and her words are a croak. 'I know.'

'Then you know I'm here because there's only one girl for me. I've known since that girl walked into my apartment and decided, for some unknown reason, that she would stay there longer than she'd stayed anywhere in fifteen years. I've known since that girl got to know me better than I know myself. Since she made me smile wider than I'd smiled before. Since she made me laugh harder than I'd ever laughed. Since she made my heart beat faster than it had ever beaten before her.'

'Jake, I can't do this.'

I take hold of her face. 'If you really can't do this, I'll be your *friend*, Jess. I'll hate that it's all you'll give me but I'll do it. I'll take what you offer because I need you in my life. But tell me honestly... that you don't love me.'

Tears run down her face and mix with the rain that falls around us. 'Jake, I'm not like you. I have nothing to offer. You have family and friends. I can't give you any of those things. And this city, this is your home. The people you love live here. I live in London, at least for now.'

I shake her gently, willing her to clear her mind. 'I have friends and family, Jess. And they love you. I don't need you to come with a side of other people. You are all I need. You are more than enough.'

Her silent tears turn to sobs and she places her hands over where mine are on her cheeks as she shakes her head.

'It's not real. This doesn't exist for me, Jake.'

I understand her words. I've heard something similar before.

'You've told me your theories of karma, Jess. You think love is out of reach? You think the way I love you, and the way I think you love me is something you can't achieve?' I take her hands and place them over my heart. 'Feel this. This is real, Jess. You feel my heart beating? It's beating for you.'

'I want...' She breaks, sobbing uncontrollably, crippled by fear.

'You want what, Jess? Talk to me.'

'I ran because I do feel it. I've fought it for as long as I can but I love you, Jake. I love you so much, it is tearing me apart.'

My arms ache to pull her into my chest. To soothe her and tell her to let this drop. But I don't.

'It's time to face your fears,' I tell her. 'Talk to me.'

Her voice breaks as she forces out the words. 'I love you so much. I love you the way my mom loved my dad. And if I let you in, we'll break. Something will happen. We'll break each other. One of us would do something, or get sick. And I...' Her words are like a fist around my heart, squeezing so tight, it could burst. 'I couldn't live without you, Jake.'

She covers her face with her hands and I finally pull her into my chest, holding her as her body crumples against me.

I wish I could take away all her years of hurt and pain. I wish I could be her strength and take away her fears. My eyes sting as I hold her, and the sky rains down on her, like it has rained down all her life. I want to be the person who stops the rain and replaces it with the light of the sun.

'Dive with me, Jess. Take my hand and dive in. We'll face everything together. I promise you that.'

She pulls out of my hold. 'We can't. Don't you see that? You could get sick or leave, or I could die and then we can't face things together.'

'Do you think I'm not afraid? Of course I am. I've never felt anything like this before. I've never felt anything this powerful. When we make love, it's like I exist in some other place, something bigger than the bed we're in, or the room, or this earth. I feel like we're bigger than the fucking universe, and that terrifies me. I can't stand here and tell you that one or both of us won't get sick. I can't promise you that we'll die holding hands in our bed together when we're eighty-five. I wish I could promise you that.'

I move to her and wipe my thumbs across the tears beneath her eyes.

'Marry me.'

She snaps her head back and her tears stop, as do her breaths, and her body's movements.

'What?'

'You heard me. You want something to hold on to? Take my heart. Take my ring. And every time you look at it you can think of this... I can't make you a promise to be by your side in this form forever. But I can vow that no matter what happens, in sickness and in health, I will forever be by your side, in this life, and the next. And, if one day, many years from now, we are up there somewhere, I will shake your father's hand, and I will kiss your mom on the cheek, and I will tell them a thousand times, "Thank you for giving me your daughter." And I'll do it all with you tucked under my arm.'

She sucks in a breath that brings her tears back.

I rub them away as I tell her, 'Marry me. Take my ring and every time you feel afraid, hold it, and know that you hold my heart. Let me be your roots, Jess. Let me be your forever home.'

She closes her eyes and for long seconds, I feel my heart stop. There's no coming back. There can be no friendship now. I put myself out there and I can't take it back. I don't want to.

She mumbles something, her eyes still closed, her tears still falling.

'What did you say?'

She opens her eyes, wide, fearful eyes, and she says, 'Yes.'

'Yes?'

'I can't promise I won't want to run. Sometimes, I might need you to stop me. I might need you to drive to Central Park and stand in the rain and tell me that all we have is hope and faith.' She lets out a short laugh that warms my whole being. 'But there's no one else in the world I want to be afraid with.'

I pull her to me and press my lips to hers, dragging my fingers through her wet hair, desperate to get more of her. I hook her legs around my waist and turn us in circles as she kisses me in a way that tells me she meant those three letters.

I'm getting married. *Married*. Me.

I couldn't be happier.

She moves her lips from mine and looks up to the sky. 'It stopped raining.'

I smile as beams of light break through the clouds. I know, wherever they are, Jess's parents are dropping in on us.

'God, I love you, Jess.'

She laughs against my mouth. 'Jake Harrington, you are a crazy, crazy kind of incredible.'

'Well, since I'm feeling kind of crazy, how does a trip to Tiffany's sound?'

'Are you sure? I mean, the proposal is a nice gesture and all but are you sure it wasn't just you being swept up in the moment? I mean, you can be a little dramatic.'

'Are you giving me grief? Seriously? After that? I swept you off your feet, Jessica Walters. That shit was like something out of the movies.'

'No, I know, it was great. I'm just saying, if you want to take it back, better sooner rather than later. Rings aren't cheap.'

I set her on the ground and press my forehead to hers. 'I'm never taking it back, babe. This is forever.'

21

JAKE

It is dark by the time we pull into Drew's driveway. I lead Jess by the hand out to the yard, where we hear the popping of corks before we see the others, sitting out on the decking by the pool.

'Hey, hey, hey! Hold the celebrations!' I shout.

We get cheers from the group and Jess and I head down to them. I make sure I'm on the right page by taking a sly look at Becky's ring finger. Happy to see a huge rock sparkling there, I pick her up and swing her around until she squeals.

'Congratulations, sis!'

'Thank you,' she giggles, clearly ecstatic.

I pull my brother into a hug. 'I'm glad you grew some balls, at last.'

He pats my back too hard in return. 'I should say the same,' he says, nodding to Jess.

I glance back at my girl as Sarah pulls her into a hug and I tell Drew, 'Yeah, you haven't heard the half of it.'

What I'm about to say is that I have some news to share with him another time, since Jess and I have decided not to trample the celebrations with our own announcement.

But...

'Oh my God! What is on your left hand?' Sarah shouts.

All attention, including mine, swings to Jess. Her cheeks burn red and she looks at Becky. 'I'm sorry, we weren't going to mention it.'

'Are you?' Becky runs to Jess and takes her hand. 'We're going to be sisters?' she squeals.

Jess laughs. 'I guess we are.'

'Show me the ring!' Madge says, running to Jess. Izzy follows suit and pretty soon the decibels coming from all the girls are seriously freaking painful.

But I'd be lying if I said I'm not bursting with happiness inside. Jess glances at me and shrugs, making me laugh, somewhere between delirium and serious damn happiness.

'You proposed?' Drew asks, humor lacing his eyes and voice. 'I thought you were just going to ask to date her, kid.'

'What can I say? If you want something, show some conviction, right?'

Laughing, he pulls me into a tight hug. 'I'm happy for you, baby brother.'

'Ah, Drew, our baby boy is all grown up,' Brooks says, throwing his arms around both mine and Drew's shoulders.

Kit shakes my hand. 'She's a catch, man. And she's willing to put up with your brooding shit. Keep her. But between us, she isn't knocked up, is she?'

'Christ, Kit, what the hell is wrong with you?' Brooks asks, clipping him on the shoulder.

Marty comes over, popping another bottle of Dom. 'Congratulations, both of you. Looks like it's the year of the Harrington brothers. In all honesty though, it was my car, wasn't it? Chicks dig the car.'

I shake my head as I fish in my pocket for his keys. 'Here. Thanks for the ride. I'll need to borrow her again tomorrow to get the scratch buffed out.'

'The... What the... Oh, no, man, you did not bump the lady.'

I shrug as I sip from my glass of champagne then set it down on the coffee table. 'It's only a scratch, Marty. It'll rub right out.'

'No, no, no. You mother...' He dives at me, hurtling both of us back into the pool. The girls scream as water splashes up over them.

'I was joking, Marty. Christ!'

For some reason, we both find it hilarious. Seemingly, so does everyone else – or they're all just high on life, too – because they all run and bomb into the pool.

I find Jess, fully clothed among the others, and lift her by the waist, raising her up out of the pool. When I bring her down, she presses her lips to mine, wraps her arms around my neck, and I take us both under the water.

22

JESS

I can hear voices as people start to arrive downstairs for Drew and Becky's engagement party. Though Jake and I intended to keep our engagement quiet, Drew and Becky insisted the party be a joint celebration. Fortunately, I brought a fancy dress with me. It's a piece from my new collection, different from my usual Asian style. It was actually inspired by Jake. I wanted to move away from always designing with an Asian feel. There's more in my life now than Asia and this dress reflects that.

Jake always has this kind of glint in his eye when I wear things off one shoulder, even my oversized shirts. So, I designed one slim shoulder strap. I made a bodice with structure but covered in black chiffon, giving a lighter appearance. The bones in the top are my roots. The layers of soft pink chiffon that flow from the true waist is the wind through my leaves.

I stare at the dress hanging on the wardrobe door as I sit on the bed in my lingerie. I'm engaged. I'm engaged to be married to Jake Harrington. I've promised to be his forever. I wait for panic to rise in my chest and to grip my lungs. I wait and wait but it doesn't come.

I glance down at my hands in my lap and realize I am gripping my beautiful ring from Tiffany's. I chose one single, brilliant-cut diamond on a thin, platinum band. Who'd have thought I'd have picked some-thing so simple? But as I stood at the counter in Tiffany's, with Jake pointing out detailed designs he thought I might like, I had a new thought. How nice it would be if life were simple.

I can't do anything to make sure life isn't turbulent, that it doesn't throw things at me I don't want to happen. But Jake somehow makes me want to stop running. I guess I knew that each time I signed another lease extension to stay with him. And when I saw him in Central Park, waiting for me in the rain, I knew I had desperately wanted him to come and find me. To root me.

I take a breath and stand. Time to put on the dress and face Jake's family.

I'm going to have a family.

A soft rap on the door steals my attention. 'Jess? It's Sarah.'

'Oh, erm, I'm in lingerie but you can come in.'

She steps inside and her lips break into one of her incredible smiles. 'You look stunning, Jess.'

'I hope you're referring to my hair and makeup because this isn't what I'm planning to wear.'

She chuckles as she comes over to me. 'Yes, I mean your hair and makeup. Jake sent me to check on you. He said you might be over-thinking a few things.'

'Well, he was probably right, but I'm fine. You look gorgeous, Sarah.' I gesture to her structured, powder-blue dress. Her hair, like mine, is curled and across one shoulder.

She waves a hand flippantly. 'This old thing? Can I help you into your dress? Is this it? I love it!'

'Thank you. It's one of mine. Jake hasn't seen it before. It's not my usual.'

'I think you're going to knock him dead. He's a real good man, you know. And he adores you.'

I try to fight my smile but it grows until my cheeks ache. 'Well, the feeling is mutual.'

She helps me into my dress. I slip my mum's pearls into my ears and around my wrist, choosing to go bare at the neck.

I add the finishing touch of a soft pink lipstick and Sarah and I look at each other in the mirror.

'Sarah, would it be weird if I said I'm pleased that Jake comes with you all as a package deal?'

She puts her arm around my shoulder. 'Not at all. We've sucked you in now and we won't let you go. And you remember what I said to you in the bar the other night. No one can promise to live forever, I know that too well. My husband was taken too young. But we can promise to *love* forever. Jake will love you forever, Jess. And so will we. If your worst fears came true, we would all be here. Neither you, nor Jake, would ever be alone. I can tell you that with certainty.'

I take a deep breath in the hope it will stop my clouded eyes from crying tears. 'I can't tell you how much... how much that...'

Sarah smiles as I hold my hand to my throat where the words are stuck. 'I know, Jess. We all do. I'll give you a minute.'

She heads downstairs and I move to the window, watching the last light of the day disappear into the ocean.

'Goodnight, Mum. Sweet dreams, Dad.' I silently thank them. They gave me my greatest fear, but they also showed me the greatest love of all. And they gave me the strength to take Jake's hand and dive in to something special.

I tried for years to run from my fear. I accept now that just because I ran from it, that didn't mean it wouldn't exist any more. And I realize fear is the thing that makes me appreciate how truly special the love my parents shared was, and how truly special the way I feel about Jake is.

With their strength, I go in search of the man I love. As I head down the stairs, I hear his laughter, that big, bellowing laugh, from outside.

I search him out and he meets my eyes, watching me as I take each step through the house and out to meet him. He looks incredible. His hair in that intentionally messy style he wears, his scruffy jaw, his blue eyes shining. His black shirt highlights his strong features and shows off the tan he's acquired over the last few days. The shirt's tucked into trousers that hug those toned hips I love to wrap my hands around. Yep, I shamelessly ogle my fiancé.

He lifts his hand to his chest as I move closer to him and that knicker-melting half smile tugs on his lips.

'Twelve,' he says when I reach him. It takes me a second to understand. 'You're a twelve. You've always been a twelve.'

The way he looks at me, like he's looking at something precious for the first time, I know he means it.

'I'm not mediocre?' I say with a giggle.

He lifts his hand to my cheek in that way he does, the way that liquefies me and tells me I'm safe all at once.

'You've never been mediocre.'

He presses his lips to mine and I can't resist slipping my tongue out to get a little of that distinctly Jake taste I love. If I could bottle his scent or design him in a new line of clothes, I would call it that: Distinctly Jake.

'Don't mind us.'

I remember where we are and pull away from Jake, subtly rubbing my lips and tucking myself into his side.

'Jess, you finally get to meet my much older sister, Millie in real life.'

Millie playfully slaps Jake in the chest before pulling me into a hug. 'So, you're the surprise sister, huh? Jake always did like to steal the stage.'

'Oh, gosh, we truly didn't mean to. It was—'

'Relax, babe. Millie is just being a dick.'

'I know you did not call your sister a name for man business.' Jake's mother, who I also recognize from Skype, spins into the little circle we're forming. 'Jess.'

She opens her arms and I step into them. Her hold is tight and warm and incredibly homey. Would it make sense if I described her as a real mum? I can't explain it better than that. She reminds me of my mum. Yes, a real mum.

'Welcome to the family, darling. I knew this was going to happen from the first time I saw him pull you onto his knee during our Sky time.'

'Enough, Mom, stop embarrassing me and let her go.' Jake pulls us apart but his mum grabs his cheeks and shakes them. It's cute as heck. 'And for the record, it's Skype. You don't Sky call.'

'Do not sass me, Jake. You're not too old to spank.'

'Christ.'

We circulate until we've met everyone. Jake's parents. His sister and her husband. Aunt Kathleen, Uncle Geoffrey, Aunt Nellie and Uncle Jack.

Staff from the catering company Drew has hired move around serving substantial canapes and making sure champagne flows. When the sky falls dark, the deck is lit by the usual lighting but also a mass of tea lights placed in the trees and woven through the trellis. It matches the sky, which is clear and full of stars. A little something I think two special people may have made happen for us, wherever they are.

An acoustic band plays at one side of the pool and the deck of the other side is used as a dance area. Aunt Kathleen and Uncle Geoffrey lead the way, dancing in each other's arms. I lean on the deck rail and watch them, my heart almost full to bursting. Some people do manage to stay in love and grow old together. Hopefully, Jake and I will be so lucky. Just in case, I make a promise to myself, in this moment, that I will live each day grateful for every second we get to share in love together.

As I have that thought, two muscular arms wrap around my waist and Jake's chin comes to rest on my shoulder. 'I love you.'

'I don't think I'll get used to or tired of you saying that to me.'

He kisses my cheek. 'Good, because I keep finding the urge to say it.'

'Jake, it's time. Let's do this,' Brooks says, dropping his hands to Jake's shoulders.

'Sorry, fiancée, I have to leave you for a few minutes. You might want to make your way down to the dance floor.'

I feel my brow scrunch as I chuckle. 'What on earth are you doing, Jake Harrington?'

'Nothing The King wouldn't do at an engagement party, babe.'

'Oh crap.'

He laughs as he and Brooks head down to the pool. The band stops mid song as Jake takes over the microphone.

'Sorry, everyone. We don't mean to disrupt proceedings but, ah, Brooks and I need to send my big brother into pre-marital life with a bang.'

Brooks hooks an electric guitar over his shoulder and Jake pics up an acoustic one.

'You ready?'

'Take it away, Elvis.'

I bring my hands to my mouth, my shoulders dancing with amusement, and the guys strike up the first chords to Elvis's 'Suspicious Minds.'

Emily's familiar voice speaks at my side. 'I knew they'd have to rock out Elvis.'

I turn to her. 'Hey! How are you? How's Brandon's nose?'

She laughs. 'He'll live. I'm so happy for you and Jake, Jess. I hope now that the guys have had their bust up, we can all hang out sometimes.'

'I'd like that. I think Jake would too.'

'Come on, girls!' Sarah sweeps in, dragging Emily and me onto the dance floor. Drew twirls Becky around, laughing when Brooks and Drew both drop to their knees, Elvis style.

Emily, Madge, Kit, Izzy, Brandon, Marty and I dance through 'Suspicious Minds' then 'All Shook Up.' Jake's parents look surprisingly young and happy as they spin around the deck.

After the two songs, Brooks calls Izzy up to the stage area. 'How about we let my man go dance, Iz?'

Izzy takes the acoustic guitar from Jake and starts playing Elvis's 'Can't Help Falling in Love.'

Everyone on the dance floor parts as Jake makes his way over to me. As he passes Brandon, he stops and I hold my breath, but he just holds out his hand. They shake. Jake then kisses Emily on the cheek. After that, he has only eyes for me.

I slip my hand into his and let him lead me into the middle of the floor. He twirls me under his arm, then brings me into his chest as Brooks and Izzy play.

He sings to me, making the lyrics his own. 'A wise man once said only fools rush in, but Jessica Walters, there wasn't a thing I could do about falling in love with you.'

'I guess some things are more powerful than you or me. Some things are bigger and stronger than all of us. I love you, Jake.'

'In this life and the next, babe.'

'In all our forms.'

He whispers, 'Forever.' And seals it with a kiss.

ABOUT THE AUTHOR

Laura Carter is the bestselling author of several rom-coms including the series *Brits in Manhattan* which she is relaunching and expanding with Boldwood. She lives in Jersey.

Sign up to Laura Carter's mailing list for news, competitions and updates on future books.

Visit Laura's website: www.lauracarterauthor.com

Follow Laura on social media:

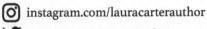 instagram.com/lauracarterauthor

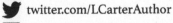 twitter.com/LCarterAuthor

 facebook.com/LauraCarterAuthor

ALSO BY LAURA CARTER

Boldwood

Boldwood Books is an award-winning fiction publishing company seeking out the best stories from around the world.

Find out more at www.boldwoodbooks.com

Join our reader community for brilliant books, competitions and offers!

Follow us
@BoldwoodBooks
@TheBoldBookClub

Sign up to our weekly deals newsletter

https://bit.ly/BoldwoodBNewsletter

Milton Keynes UK
Ingram Content Group UK Ltd.
UKHW041110171023
430768UK00001B/1